HACKNEY CENTRAL

BY

MICHAEL K FOSTER

DEDICATION

In Memory of
Malcolm Frazer Scott

.

By
Michael K Foster

DCI Jack Mason Crime Thriller Series:

THE WHARF BUTCHER

SATAN'S BECKONING

THE SUITCASE MAN

CHAMELEON

THE POACHER'S POCKET

Novella

HACKNEY CENTRAL (*Beginnings*)

ACKNOWLEDGMENTS

All my DCI Mason and David Carlisle novels are works of fiction based in the North East of England. There are so many people without whose help and support it would have been difficult, if not impossible, to write with any sense of authenticity. Suffering from dyslexia as I do, my grateful thanks go out to the late Rita Day and my dear wife Pauline, whose belief and inspiration has never waned.

I am indebted to Detective Constable Maurice Waugh, a former member of the Yorkshire Ripper Squad, and Ken Stewart, a former member of South Shields CID. Their technical assistance of how the police tackle crime has allowed me a better understanding of what takes place. Their efforts have helped me enormously.

To single out a few other names who helped make a difference to the book, I would like to thank Robert Barnes and Lynn Oakes for their encouragement and unqualified support in developing the initial cover graphics. Finally, I would express my heartfelt appreciation to the Beta reader team: Jan Duffy, Maria Jones, Mark Duffy, Daniel Inman, and Brenda Forster, without whose help this book would never have made the bookshelf.

Michael K Foster
Co Durham England
www.mickaelkfoster.com

CHAPTER

ONE

He didn't know any of them, but he knew their smell: cannabis, trouble and arrogance. Ignoring the unmistakable "herbal" whiff, Detective Sergeant Jack Mason stepped into the steel sarcophagus, pressed the ground-floor button, and waited for the lift doors to close. Ten floors up on the **Clapton Park Estate** wasn't the safest environment to be in, not at any time. These thugs didn't have a conscience, but they certainly had balls. Either way, this was his domain and he was determined to make his presence felt.

Looking around, there was something unnerving about his fellow passengers, as if they knew who'd turned old Harold Watkins' flat over. Left for dead on his living room floor, the level of violence used was deplorable and totally needless.

As the lift began its descent, he could hear the machinery creaking and the cables whipping in the shaft. Above the door, hidden amongst the graffiti, he noticed a green digital display counting down the floor levels. Fast descents spooked him. It felt unnatural, as though he was plummeting to earth and certain death.

1

'You people from around here?' Mason asked, knowing full-well they weren't.

'What's it to you, motherfucker?'

He was seventeen, no more. Still capable, nevertheless.

Clearly the ringleader, the sergeant sized him up. He wore a crew-neck T-shirt tight across the chest, blue jeans and a pair of white Reebok trainers, loosely laced. Mason had seen his like too many times over the years. Gangs were part of the inner-city fabric these days, and few neighbourhoods were crime-free. Many observers maintained that poverty, sub-standard housing, and unemployment were the cause of the problem, but there was a lot more to it. Gangs were relatively sophisticated organisations, built on loyalty, trust, and the basic need of feeling wanted. Where society had failed miserably to provide facilities in which young people could attach themselves, gang masters had given them hope.

The sergeant's stare hardened. 'Not seen you people around here before.'

'So what?' a youth with short-cropped hair replied.

'And you are?' Mason asked.

'Keep your nose out, or else.'

Tension hung in the air. Intimidating.

Mason moved from the back of the lift towards the door. A precautionary measure, he wasn't giving in to bullying tactics. Not now. Not at any time. Show signs of weakness and these scoundrels would beat him to within an inch of his life. Supremacy ruled here, it was the fabric on which the estate had been built. Gang leaders ruled with an iron fist, and residents feared for their lives and were too frightened to speak out. Even the police patrolled in numbers. Never alone. The trouble was, gangs who formed alliances with one another only brought more misery to the streets. It was a never-ending cycle, and no one could put a stop to it.

Not until now that is.

The moment he felt the floor shake under his feet and the doors opening, the sergeant made his move. He was quick, too quick, and as he stepped out of the lift, he turned sharply to confront them.

'Where do you lot live?' he demanded.

Confused at first, the ringleader slid his hand inside his pocket, trying to conceal the motion. Mason knew what was hidden there and shifted the weight to the balls of his feet. A melting pot for knife crime, two homicides had been linked to local gangs in the past two months. GBH was commonplace, and nine local gang members had recently been jailed for violent street robbery.

He heard the menacing click of a knife blade opening and froze.

'I warned you to keep your fucking nose out of it,' the ringleader snarled.

'Don't make this hard for yourself.'

'Oh yeah? And who's gonna come to your rescue now?'

'Give him it, Tony!' another yelled out.

As the knot in his stomach tightened, the sergeant clenched his fists in readiness. In what was a well-rehearsed routine, the six troublemakers now circled him. He'd been here before, many times, and knew what

3

damage these bastards could inflict on a person. Six against one wasn't the greatest odds, but his mind was already made up. He would take the ringleader out first – a size nine boot to the crotch.

Right on cue, a marked Ford Sierra GLS appeared out of nowhere, barely fifty metres away, the officers inside speeding to his assistance, shifting the odds rapidly in his favour. The thugs took off towards the concrete jungle, and the air felt much sweeter suddenly.

'You all right?' the young constable called out, as he slid from the moving vehicle and ran to Mason's assistance.

'I'm fine,' he replied, holding up his warrant card. 'Who are they?'

'Never seen them before, Sarge. Do you want me to follow them?'

'No. They're probably miles away by now.'

The constable shrugged, as if waiting for further instructions.

Mason thanked them and pocketed his warrant card. Too late now, he thought, he'd deal with it later. Whoever the ringleader was, he now had a name. It wasn't much, but it was enough. These scoundrels wouldn't be too difficult to find, it was just a matter of legwork. The problem was an old man lay dying in a hospital bed and his flat had been ransacked. Whoever was responsible for such a heinous crime needed to be brought to justice, and fast.

He glanced at the marked police car as it slid from the estate, then up at the tower block again. With any luck the police surgeon Dr White, along with the Scenes of Crime Officers, would report their findings before long. If not, his weekend would slip away from him like so many others had in the past.

CHAPTER TWO

It was late afternoon when Jack Mason finally arrived back at Hackney Central Police station, a red brick construction on Lower Clapton Road in the heart of London's East End. Recently promoted to the Metropolitan's Serious Crime Squad, Mason was loving every minute of it. *Detective Sergeant!* his wife Brenda had shrieked the moment he broke the news to her. She was so proud of him, so excited, and he'd always dreamt of heading up his own investigation team. Now one step closer, he was definitely out to impress.

The office was open plan, high-ceilinged, with canted bay windows overlooking Clapton Square and the busy A107. Compared to other divisions in the capital, there was always plenty to do here. It was a large catchment area, and the crime rate for the Borough of Hackney was considered by many to be slightly above average. Mason felt at home here and worked with a great bunch of like-minded officers who were eager to get things done.

The sergeant closed the office door behind him still grappling with the notion of the Clapton Park knife attack. He'd been lucky, of course, and had got off relatively lightly, considering. Still, he was eager to find out who 'Tony' was and determined to get even. Not today, though: he'd promised to take Brenda out for a slap-up birthday meal and he was really looking forward to that.

Mason groaned as he stared at the mountain of paperwork covering his desk. Forms were the bane of every police officer's life, and they were spreading like the bubonic plague. Too much emphasis had been placed on accountability nowadays, and not enough energy channelled into fighting crime. Everyone was pissed off by it, and something had to give.

Ignoring the steady stream of incoming calls, Mason finished his incident report and checked his in-tray. The only positive news he could offer, was that forensics had finally finished their investigations into Harold Watkins' flat. It wasn't much, but it was a start. Still unable to interview the old man, the team were having to work blind. Not the best approach to solving a crime, but there wasn't a lot they could do about it.

The sergeant sat for a moment and tried to get his head around it all. Most crimes followed a distinct pattern, but Mason was in a quandary. Was this a planned attack or the work of an opportunist? he wondered.

Mason caught his companion's eye. 'Any feedback from our door-to-door enquiries?'

Norwell Summers, a thirty-four-year-old detective lifted his head above the divider screen and smiled. He had a casual, unruffled approach which Mason always found reassuring.

'Nothing yet, Sarge.'

'What about uniforms? Any more reports of local troublemakers on the Clapton Park Estate?'

'No. Nothing of interest has shown up.'

Mason shuffled awkwardly. 'That's odd. I could have sworn someone would have seen or heard something, especially the amount of damage that was done to the flat.'

'People are scared to talk,' Norwell frowned, 'and I can't say that I blame them.'

Mason grunted his agreement. This was a particularly nasty attack, but it wasn't the first time it had happened on the estate. There were others. Too many if truth be told. Then again, it was always difficult to carry out a stop and search operation, never mind the dangers involved.

Mason looked at his watch.

'What about local gang fights? Anything in the overnights?'

'There was a bit of a punch up over at the Prince of Wales yesterday evening, which spilled out into Millfields Park.' Summers handed him a printout of the incident report. 'Two gangs fighting over territorial rights apparently.'

'Drugs, no doubt?'

'Difficult to say. According to the duty officers present, there were three arrests for disturbance of the peace, two broken windows, and a few cuts and bruises. Other than that, no one was seriously injured.'

Mason wasn't surprised by the detective constable's answer. Street gangs often covered a few blocks of an estate, while higher-level criminal factions controlled large swathes of it. That's how an area was divided up, how it was controlled. The danger was when a small gang formed an alliance with another, it morphed into a larger organisation and invariably spelled trouble. It was all about domination, and ever since the introduction of crack cocaine onto the estate, new territory was being hard fought over. What followed was a deplorable series of events, and one that was difficult to prevent.

The sergeant cocked his head to one side. 'This recent spate of attacks on old people's flats sounds as if someone is trying to escalate up the criminal ladder.'

'Could be. But why pick on **defenceless** pensioners?'

'Vulnerable targets, I presume?'

'Possible, but highly unlikely, don't you think?'

'I'm still not convinced. The problem is high-level drug dealers usually control large chunks of the city using enforcers who are able to make money under the additional protection of their supplier.' Mason crinkled his brow. 'The question is, who's running the estate?'

'Do you think Harold Watkins' property was deliberately targeted?'

'I'm not convinced it was a group of youths who turned his flat over, if that's what you're thinking. This was about inflicting fear onto the estate – an attempt to keep a tight lid on things.'

Summers rocked back in his seat. 'I wonder if someone is using young hooligans as a cover-up for their own activities?'

'Anything's possible. The problem with that is, there's very little in the way of fingerprints, no eyewitness accounts, and nobody is willing to talk.'

Summers conceded with a shrug. 'True––'

'Well, then?'

'You may have a point, Sarge. But my money is on a local gang being involved.'

Mason cut Summers short by raising his hand. 'You know what a group of teenagers are like once they're let loose on a property. They egg each other on, cause unnecessary wilful damage and always stamp their mark on it. What's more, there was no graffiti left on the walls which you'd expect to find from a group of seasoned hooligans.'

The constables frown lines tightened again. 'Someone had it in for the old man, that is for sure.'

Summers had a point, and a good one at that. Whoever had threatened him at knifepoint had rattled his cage. He would need to find out who 'Tony' was, establish what he and his band of cronies were up to around the time the Watkin's attack took place. Could they be part of a distraction tactic as Summers was suggesting, or just a group of local scrotes intent on causing trouble?

The man leading the investigations approached from a side room.

'What's the latest on the Harold Watkins break in?' DCI Cummins asked.

'He's still in intensive care,' Mason replied, dutifully.

'We need to get a statement from him, the sooner the better in this case.'

'I'll call by at the hospital in the morning, Boss.'

'Good man. Let's hope he's made a full recovery by then and is able to give us a few answers.'

Bob Cummins was old school. Now nearing retirement, his thirty-five years' in the Metropolitan Police were slowly coming to an end. Known throughout the station as "Boss", Mason had warmed to the title. It had a nice ring to it, not overly condescending compared to sir! Cummins was a down-to-earth police officer and wasn't pretentious like some of the other senior officers he knew. He was astute, unwavering, and eager to share a lifetime's knowledge with anyone willing to listen. Deep down he reminded him of Ralph Curtis, an old family friend and ex-police officer who had taken him under his wing after his father had left home. Mason decided that if ever he rose to the dizzy heights of DCI, he too would be addressed as "Boss".

Cummins shook his head in despair. 'Our suspect's local, I'm convinced of that.'

'What, you think Harold Watkins knew his attacker?'

'If not, he knew someone who did.'

Mason raised an eyebrow. 'What makes you say that?'

'No signs of breaking and entering, Sergeant. It's as simple as that.'

'Possible, but I'm––'

'Let's sleep on it, see what the old man has to say to you in the morning.'

Glancing round, the DCI turned on his heels and disappeared through the main office door. Thank God for that, Mason smiled. No more chasing around looking for witness statements tonight. As usual, it had been a tiring day, and he was really looking forward to his evening out with Brenda. He still hadn't made his mind up where they would eat – but he was working on it.

CHAPTER THREE

Jack Mason entered Hackney Central in sombre mood the next morning. The news of Harold Watkins' untimely death had hit home hard. It wasn't often a murder victim got to him, but this crime had left a nasty taste in his mouth. Beaten about the head without ever gaining consciousness wasn't exactly the nicest way to die, not in anyone's books. What his family would make of it, Mason dreaded to think. All the old man's worldly possessions had been stolen, and his flat ransacked.

Speed was key. Whoever had carried out such a despicable act would be keen to shift their ill-gotten gains. That's how these crimes usually worked, especially in London. There were dozens of black-market outlets he could think of, and any one of them would know how to handle the old man's stolen possessions. It was all about contacts, striking the right deal, and finding the right outlets to shift your spoils. Many were legitimate businesses, or "fronts" as they were better known. The problem was once stolen property hit the black market it was virtually impossible to trace.

It had taken Jack Mason a little over an hour to set the complex machinery of a murder enquiry in motion. It was now eleven o'clock, and once they'd gathered enough hard evidence regarding the victim's last known movements, it would be a simple matter of pulling a plan together. This wasn't a spontaneous attack on a vulnerable pensioner, this crime was organised – as if the intruder knew what he was looking for.

The Briefing Room was small, low ceilinged, with two sash windows overlooking the main carpark. As usual there was a mad scramble for seats. Ten straight-backed chairs laid out in a single row in front of an incident corkboard, the rest of the team standing shoulder to shoulder at the back of the room.

Hands deep in pockets, Mason felt a ripple of excitement as he stood in front of the assembled team. The mechanics of a murder investigation could be quite daunting at times, but he was keen that *Operation Cello* got off to a good start. He guessed there were about twenty officers crammed in here – forensics, SOCOs, road traffic, CID, uniformed police officers – most of them familiar, and a few hoping for their first big break. The only person missing was DCI Cummins, who had been summoned at short notice to Superintendent Smyth's office for a progress update.

The room fell silent.

'Okay,' Mason began. 'Around 5.00 pm, on January 22nd, two officers were called to a house burglary over on Clapton Park Estate after a neighbour reported a male occupant was lying face down on his living room floor. When the Emergency Services arrived at the scene, they found an 82 year-pensioner suffering from serious head wounds. Taken to Homerton University Hospital, he was put on a life support machine but died from his injuries in the early hours of this morning.'

'I take it the press are already aware of the incident?' said DC Jones, an astute forward-thinking detective in his late twenties.

'Yes. They are.'

'Pity,' Jones replied, shaking his head. 'Do we know what other injuries the victim sustained?'

'Apart from serious head wounds, he suffered three broken ribs, severe bruising to the neck and back, and minor lacerations to his face and upper limbs. This was a particularly vicious attack, which poses an obvious increase of danger to the wider public.' Mason waited for the noise levels to die down before continuing. 'What I can tell you is, the victim's name is Harold Watkins. Well-known locally, Watkins worked in London's docklands for a number of years.'

'Having read the initial reports,' said DC Summers, 'I take it only one person was involved in the actual attack?'

'That's correct.' Mason took a deep breath. 'Let's not jump to conclusions at this stage, not until we see what the coroner's report throws up.'

'Could others be involved?'

'They could, but according to forensics they never entered the flat.'

'What about immediate neighbours?' Evans from CID asked. 'Did anyone see or hear anything?'

'Not to my knowledge they didn't.' Mason rolled his eyes and shrugged. 'The problem is, no one is willing to come forward and we're faced with a wall of silence.'

'Fear of reprisals more like,' Evans replied.

Mason glanced at his notes. Forensics had revealed very little about the perpetrator. There were no witness statements, few fingerprints, and very little in the way of hard evidence. These things took time, he realised that, but the media's insatiable demand for answers would soon rear its ugly head.

He chose his next words carefully.

'According to the police doctor's report, we know the attack took place between the hours of 10:30 am and 11:30 am on Wednesday 22nd. This means the victim had lain unconscious for at least five hours before he was finally discovered.'

'Any word back on the murder weapon?' one of the senior detectives cut in.

'Nothing yet.' Mason narrowed his eyes a fraction. 'Initial reports indicate that blunt force trauma to the back of the head was the probable cause of death. In my view a heavy wooden object was used – a baseball or cricket bat, something of that nature.'

John Chambers, a dapper Detective Constable in his late thirties and former Essex County cricket player, raised a hand. Around six foot-one, he was a good four inches taller than Jack Mason. 'What about CCTV coverage?' asked Chambers, pointing up at the street map. 'Do we have any in the area?'

Constable Summers was quick to react. 'Nothing of interest has shown up, but uniforms are still working on it.'

'No word from the lab on the fingerprints yet?' Mason asked.

'Later today, Sarge. They're hoping to find a match on the database.'

DC John Callum, a balding, eagle-eyed detective waved his hand in the air. 'This gold presentation watch that is known to have gone missing during the attack. What more do we know about that?'

Mason turned sharply to Callum after drawing the team's attention to a photograph pinned to the corkboard. 'As far as we know, it's a man's gold Vacheron Constantin wristwatch very similar to this one. Presented to Watkins on the day of his retirement, we know his name was engraved on the back of it, so it shouldn't be difficult to identify.'

Callum shrugged. 'If it's easily identifiable, surely it will have been melted down for its scrap value by now.'

'That would seem the most obvious way to dispose of it,' another agreed.

'Let's not get carried away,' Mason said, firmly. 'This is an extremely valuable watch, and any number of dodgy East End pawn brokers would take it on, no questions asked.'

'In other words, find the watch and it could lead us back to our suspect.'

'Exactly,' Mason replied.

Summers sounded surprised. 'Hang on a minute. If the old man was wearing it at the time of the attack, it must have been taken from his wrist at some point.'

Mason nodded. 'That's true—'

'Seems funny. If this wasn't planned, we could be looking at an opportunist here.'

Mason dug his hands in his pockets as he stared out of the office window. The constable was right, Watkins never let it out of his sight according to close friends. It was a prized possession, a lifetime's memories spent working in the London Docks. No, Mason thought, whoever stole it obviously knew its true value. The more he thought about it, the more aggravated robbery sprang to mind. Friendships ran deep, and unsolved murders never rested kindly on a comrade's mind – let alone give closure. Surely someone would come forward if they ever spotted it again.

Mason pointed to a map of the Clapton Park Estate. 'There's been a lot of complaints lately regarding local youths making a nuisance of themselves on the estate. I want a list of their names, and anyone else seen in the vicinity around the time the attack took place.'

'What about known housebreakers?' asked DC Callum.

'I was coming to that,' the sergeant answered firmly.

His response provoked an enthusiastic murmur, as a flurry of potential candidate's names were floated about. This wasn't as easy as Mason had first thought, and the questions were coming thick and fast. There were plans to set in motion, interviews to arrange, and dozens of suspects to be put under the microscope.

'Okay,' Mason said, looking at his watch. 'DCI Cummins will be holding a full team briefing later this afternoon, so let's pull a list together of all the likely candidates.'

As the meeting drew to a close, Mason turned to Summers and said, 'Fancy a drink?'

The constable looked at him confused. 'Not whilst I'm on duty, Sarge.'

'Who said anything about a pub?'

'I know how your mind works – that's why I'm a detective.'

Mason grabbed his coat. 'It's time we paid a few local watering holes a visit.'

'Anywhere in particular?'

'Let's start with the Clapton Hart and see what develops from there.'

'Walking distance, eh?'

'The exercise will do you good, Norwell.'

'Just because I'm six years older than you doesn't mean I'm not fit.'

Mason smiled at the constable's spontaneous remark. Now nearing twenty-eight himself, his years in the Metropolitan had taught him many things. Above all, never to take anything for granted.

***

The Clapton Hart was quiet, Thursday lunchtime being one of the lowest points of the week. A friendly pub, over the centuries it had traded as a stagecoach inn, guest house, and on several occasions a lively nightclub. Many a dodgy deal had been struck inside these premises and Mason was well aware of the clientele who frequented it.

'How's tricks, Reggie?' Mason said, by way of introduction.

The barman looked up from behind the bar and smiled. 'Not a lot happening if I'm honest, Jack.'

'When's payday?'

'Tomorrow, and this place will be rocking again.'

A man in his late fifties, Reggie Brown had been a regular barman at the Clapton Hart for as long as Mason could remember. Not a fit man, portly, with a large forehead and receding hairline, he had a broad Cockney accent.

'If it's food you're wanting, the best I can offer is a bag of crisps.'

'Better make it two pints of lager, and two bags of salt and vinegar!'

'We've run out of salt and vinegar.'

'Cheese and onion will do.'

The barman reached inside a cardboard box and smiled. 'You're in luck. It's the last two packets.'

Mason pointed to the mute television fixed to the back wall. 'Football fan, Reggie?'

'I like to watch the odd match now and again, and you?'

'I'm a rugby man mainly... London Wasps.'

'That's over in Sudbury isn't it?

Mason sheepishly grinned. 'It is.'

'So, what's the attraction with London Wasps?'

The sergeant took a long swig of his lager and stepped back a pace. 'Many years ago, I was listening to a live match on the radio. It was the quarter finals of the cup and Wasps were playing Bath. It's amazing how some things can grab your attention when you're twelve-years old. The mere mention of *Wasps,* and I was hooked.' Mason wiped the froth from his lips and slid the half empty glass on the bar. 'I've followed them ever since. Even watched their first appearance in the John Player Cup knock-out competition back in eighty-six.'

The barman stared at him but said nothing.

Mason frowned. 'They were beaten by Bath, 25 points to 17.'

'Not a good day then?'

Mason ran the flat of his hand over the top of his head as he leaned over, thinking. 'I heard the old guy who was attacked over on the Clapton Park Estate died early this morning.'

'That's sad,' the barman sighed. 'I was hoping he'd pull through.'

'Did you know him?'

'Not really.'

'He drank here, I presume?'

'Not in a long time.' The barman cocked his head to one side. 'Mind, a couple of regulars were talking about him only last night.'

'Oh. What did they say?'

'Heard it was a couple of yobs. Wouldn't surprise me. Been getting worse on the estate. Bloody teenagers ain't scared of authority. That's the problem.'

Mason stared into his now empty pint glass and tried not to make eye contact. 'Young hooligans? I hadn't heard about that.'

The barman nodded sourly. 'Yeah, kids picking on innocent bystanders for no reason at all.'

Mason wrinkled his nose. 'Soft targets by the sounds–'

'More likely than not. Same everywhere. Stratford's rife with it. All these kids using the A12 to go to other parts of town to mug people, it ain't good.'

'Sounds like the old Scottish border raids if you ask me.'

The barman's brow corrugated. 'God knows. It's getting out of hand and it's time the police put a stop to it.'

Summers lifted his glass and stopped just short of his lips. 'Stratford is rife with it, you say?'

'Yeah, so I heard.'

'First I've heard of it,' said Mason. 'Mind, I did hear there's been bother over at the Prince of Wales pub lately. I wonder if it's connected?'

'Possibly the same bunch of yobs from Stratford.' The barman looked at them and pointed. 'Can I get you two gentleman another drink?'

'Same again for me,' Mason replied. 'What about you, Norwell?'

The constable looked down at his empty glass and grimaced. 'No thanks. Not whilst I'm on––' he stopped mid-sentence realising what he was about to say.

'What about a half then?' Mason said, beaming like a Cheshire cat.

'Better make it my last, as I've got a busy afternoon ahead of me.'

'Haven't we all!'

CHAPTER
FOUR

Jack Mason was sitting in his favourite armchair, sipping a Talisker single malt whisky watching 'The X-Files' on TV. Curled up beside him, Brenda was flipping through a baby catalogue and looking for blankets to go with the new "4-wheel travel system" she'd spotted in Mothercare. Mindful of the consultant gynaecologist's advice that she would need to take it easy over the next few weeks, they'd limited their nights out together to just once a week. Tuesday, quiz night, down at their local pub where they could chat and relax amongst friends.

As he let his mind drift, Mason remembered how they'd first met. He was on his way to the airport, funnily enough, having shared a taxi with Brenda. Within minutes of meeting they'd ended up talking about their previous holiday experiences. Not that he was looking for a relationship at the time, he wasn't. He preferred his own company if he was honest. Being single fitted nicely with his manly social activities, and he wasn't prepared to make the sacrifices. But life was full of surprises, and within weeks of exchanging telephone numbers, they'd arranged to meet over dinner one night. In Knightsbridge of all places, an upmarket Italian restaurant near Harvey Nichols which had cost him an arm and a leg.

A few years younger than him, Brenda was easy to get on with. An attractive young woman, she was intelligent, charming, and above all wasn't put off by his being a police officer. Within weeks of them hitting it off, they slowly realised that theirs wasn't just a casual relationship. There was something more serious going on. Mason had never shared his secrets with another woman before, and this was all new ground to him. But Brenda was perfect – and he couldn't have chosen a better person to spend the rest of his days with had he tried.

After a whirlwind honeymoon in the Caribbean, they had no plans to have children. Not straight away they hadn't. At the time, Brenda was working as a Personal Assistant for an internationally recognised property development and investment company in central London and was doing really well. Nine months later, when Brenda was pregnant with a baby girl, they bought a smart little two-bedroom property near Tower Hamlets. It hadn't been easy, though, but thanks to some hard graft and a ten thousand-pound bank overdraft, they'd somehow managed to turn a small back room into a nursery and decorated it from top to bottom. Proud of his DIY handiwork, Mason had altered the kitchen layout, fitted dimmer switches and low-level lighting in every room. With everything falling into place before the baby was due, a new drop side cot had arrived, together with a wide chest of drawers. The height was perfect for changing a baby according to Brenda, who believed it would provide ample future storage space for clothes.

Not all had gone to plan, though. Choosing the perfect name had been their biggest nightmare, as they could not agree on anything. Brenda was keen on Janet Alison, but when Mason pointed out the initials spelt out JAM, she immediately scuppered the idea. They'd eventually settled for Catherine, but neither liked the shortened version nor found a suitable replacement.

'So, what have you been up to today?' Brenda asked.

'Not a lot. We've been looking for a stolen watch.'

'So, that's what you get up to all day!'

'That amongst other things.'

Brenda gave Mason a puzzled look. 'What type of watch is it?'

'It's a Vacheron Constantine Geneve wristwatch.'

'It sounds more like an Italian seaside resort to me. What's so important about it?'

'We believe it was taken from the victim's wrist after he'd lain unconscious in his flat for several hours.'

'This wouldn't be the pensioner over on Clapton Park, would it? The one who was recently murdered.'

'Yes, it was.'

Brenda raised her eyebrows a fraction. 'It shouldn't be too difficult a case to solve by the sounds. Find the watch, and you'll find your culprit.'

'You should have been a detective, darling.' Mason placed a reassuring hand on Brenda's swollen stomach and could feel the baby moving inside. 'Bambi's active tonight.'

'The minute I put my feet up she kicks off again. It happens every time, especially during the night. She seems determined to let me know who's the boss around here.'

'Sounds like a typical woman. . . trying to get the last word in.'

Brenda managed a thin, wintery smile. 'You better get used to the idea, Jack, as you'll soon have two women to contend with around the house.'

'Wall to wall stereophonic women talk – I can't wait.'

As he drifted into the kitchen to make some supper, he blew Brenda a kiss. Mason was quite looking forward to becoming a dad and couldn't wait for the big day to arrive. Never in a million years did he think he would warm to the idea, but it couldn't come soon enough as far as he was concerned.

'What do you fancy for supper?'

'I've opened a fresh jar of pickled onions,' Brenda shouted through the open doorway.

'So I see. How many this time?'

'Better make it a large spoonful, any more gives me indigestion!'

Mason smiled resignedly to himself. It was weird how pregnant women suddenly developed a craving for some foods. Brenda's passion was pickled onions dipped in peanut butter, and she couldn't get enough of them. Thankfully it wasn't cheese, as her dietitian had warned that mould-ripened soft cheeses can contain bacteria that may harm the baby. He'd read somewhere that some cravings, such as sour foods like lemons, pickles, or salty foods were a pregnant woman's body's way of getting a variety of nutrients the baby needed. How much of it was true he had no idea, but he was sure as hell confused by it all.

'I've been thinking about this murder enquiry you're now involved in,' Brenda shouted through.

'What about it?'

'How involved are you?'

'It's still early days, but the man leading the investigation has told me I'm to head up my own small investigation team.'

There followed a long pause.

'They *will* give you paternity leave once our baby arrives, won't they?'

'I'm hoping we've caught the killer by then, darling. Besides, there are plenty of other good officers who can step into my shoes once Bambi arrives.'

'I hope you're not just saying it to appease me.'

'Of course not. What makes you think I'd do such a thing?'

'I know you of old Jack, and you've been working a lot more overtime since your promotion to Detective Sergeant.'

'It just seems that way, darling. I can assure you I'm not.'

'Well,' Brenda sighed. 'It certainly seems like I'm spending an awful lot more time on my own lately.'

Mason felt his stomach lurch. This was the first murder investigation he'd been put in charge of a small team of detectives, and he was determined to make a good start. Failure wasn't an option, and God forbid someone else stepping into his shoes at this critical stage in the investigations. It didn't bear thinking about.

Returning from the kitchen he gripped Brenda's hand, firmly but gently. 'I know there's a lot going on in our lives at the moment, but once Bambi arrives everything will fall into place.'

Brenda screwed her face up. 'I've heard that somewhere before, Jack.'

'It's true. I promise you——'

'Try pulling the other leg.'

'What makes you say that?'

'Once you get your teeth stuck into something, you're like a dog with a bone. You can't stand failure, Jack, and never could.'

Mason squeezed Brenda's hand and gave her a loving smile. 'Trust me, darling. The minute Bambi arrives I'll be out of my office quicker than a rabbit out of a magician's hat.'

Brenda gave him a suspicious look. 'Really?' she replied.

Chapter Five

Tony Abbott, the Southside Gang leader, peered out through the gap in the bedroom window blinds just as another police van pulled into the street. This was the third in as many hours, and he was furious. The police were everywhere, and their stop and search tactics on the estate screwed everything up, making life a misery. These next few hours would be crucial if they were ever going to take back control of the streets. So many questions, so much uncertainty, it was driving him mad. He would meet with his counterpart on the northside of the estate and negotiate a truce. It would be difficult. He knew that, but nothing was ever simple on the Clapton Park Estate especially now the Metropolitan had taken back control.

Abbott punched the number into his phone and waited for a connection.

'Yeah,' the voice on the other end of the phone snarled.

'We need to talk.'

'About what?'

The North Boys leader wasn't the friendliest person on earth to deal with, not at any time. The man had attitude and wouldn't think twice about slitting his throat if he felt it would enhance his street credibility. He would need to tread carefully, be patient, and win the idiot over to his way of thinking.

'It's the filth,' Abbot replied.

'What about them?'

'The whole of Southside is crawling with them. Dogs everywhere, stop and search teams on every street corner, you name it, it's happening.'

'Same here,' came back the muted reply.

'Well?'

'Well what?'

'If we don't act soon, we'll go into meltdown,' the Southside Gang leader said, in the toughest voice he could muster.

Another long pause.

'Like shit. Anyone who steps out of line on my patch knows what to expect.'

'It ain't about muscle anymore, bruv. I've heard rumours.'

'About what?'

'Can't say over the phone. That's why we need to talk.'

'Meet me in Ronnie's Coffee Bar in fifteen minutes. . . alone.'

Abbott's phone went dead.

Frustrated, the Southside Gang leader stared out of the window, thinking. Ever since the old man over in Ambergate Court popped his clogs the estate had gone into lockdown. No one could move in or out without the police knowing about it. It wasn't good, and it was time to put a stop to it.

Wearing his trademark hoodie, blue jeans, and white trainers tied loose, Abbott shuffled awkwardly towards the bathroom landing. He was craving for a fix, something to settle his nerves and take his mind off outside influences. Frustrated by the number of police officers roaming the estate, he was totally pissed off. They were the real enemy, and the worst thing anyone could possibly do was to cooperate with them. But people talked, and you never knew who might say something when the chips were down. Knocking on your door in the middle of the night was the Metropolitan's favourite pastime. Unnecessary bad shit.

Abbott had decided against carrying a blade. Far too risky, he thought. The last thing he would need would be to be hauled into a police station and his dabs taken. Most gang members' names were already on file, and many were proud of it. The problem was, whenever they dragged you into the Nick for questioning you never knew what charges they might throw at you. The police were unpredictable.

Shuffling downstairs, the kitchen door was on the latch. He eased it open just as another police van crept into view. Of all the police officers, he hated the dog handler teams most. Dangerous bastards. Vicious. Once they let the hounds on you anything could happen – and usually did. They could bite you in the nuts, rip off your arm, and bring you to ground in the blink of an eye. If he had a shooter, he would blow their brains out, and live the rest of his life in peace.

'Well, maybe.'

As the K-9 van crawled past him at a snail's pace, Abbott froze. The filth inside looked docile enough, but you never could tell with these bastards. Faking it was commonplace, and showing disinterest was another favourite trick they used. Then again, they were probably listening to radio two. If not, they'd be twiddling with their Rubik's cubes trying to get the colours to match.

'*Dumb bastards,*' he cursed.

Once the K-9 van had disappeared, the Southside Gang leader shrugged down in his hoodie and slipped into the street. This was his patch, his domain, and no one was ever going to take it from him. The trouble was his plan to get the police off his back hadn't worked, and he'd been holed up inside his bedroom far too long. How would he convince Zelly their territory was now under threat? Would he even listen?

***

It was nine o'clock, and there were dozens of vehicles parked up outside Ronnie's Coffee Bar. A few he recognised, others he'd never seen before. His hoodie pulled low over his face, Abbott hung around in the newsagent's doorway and waited. The chances of being spotted here were slim, but sometimes the police got lucky. He would keep a low profile, bide his time, and move when the coast was clear.

He lit up a cigarette he'd nicked from his mother's kitchen drawer and blew out a long smoke trail. The coffee bar was full and his counterpart was occupying a window seat and playing to the crowd. Was he carrying a blade?

Twenty feet to his left, two men were staring out of a long wheel-based transit van. One was mid-forties and fat, the other scrawny and older. Dressed in blue overalls, open neck shirts, and looking decidedly pissed off, he guessed they were workmen. They could be police officers in disguise of course, or undercover informants making life difficult. Maybe not, Abbott thought. Besides, he could smell rats a zillion miles away, and these two bastards smelled clean.

Seconds later, he was inside and staring across at his arch enemy.

'Took your time,' the North Boys leader's voice boomed out.

'What are you banging on about?'

'This better be good, cos I've got deals on hold.'

Abbott scooted his chair. This wasn't the kind of place that was listed in any of the tourist guides, but at least it was neutral ground. No Man's Land stuck in the middle of the estate and separating the two warring factions from serious trouble. Today felt different, though. Something menacing hung in the air, a threat to their territories.

Abbott looked at Zelly, who nodded. 'What have you heard, bruv?'

'I was about to ask you that same question, dumb mother fucker.'

Brian Fagan, aka Zelly, was a year older than him. Much taller, more physical. Not the nicest person to hang out with. If the man had half a brain, he'd realise his territory was under threat. He didn't, and that was Abbott's dilemma. Zelly was thick-skinned, pig-headed, and ruled the North Boys with an iron fist. And that was another concern that had crossed Abbott's mind that morning. How to win Zelly over?

Zelly had attitude, and a huge ego to go with it. It was all about posture, strutting your stuff and making your opponent feel inferior.

'I've heard rumours,' Abbott said, through gritted teeth.

'About what?'

'The filth are looking for the scumbag who killed the old geezer over in Ambergate Court.'

Zelly's eyes narrowed a fraction. 'Nothing for you to worry about then.'

'Don't shit me. The suspect came from your neck of the woods.'

'Well it ain't one of us, so it must be one of you.'

Abbott hunched his shoulders in a show of contempt.

'What if someone's trying to stitch the two of us up?'

'Who?'

'How the fuck would I know?'

Zelly's eyes flashed like daggers. 'What are you prattling on about?'

Suddenly, Zelly's hands were under the table and the room held its breath as the door opened and a known troublemaker named 'Bixby' swaggered in. A local lowlife, with a barbed-wire tattoo round his neck and a mouth full of rotten teeth, the man was known for looking for fights.

Bixby's small, flat eyes fixed on Zelly. 'Yow.'

Abbot saw the knife, Zelly's knife, its menacing long blade was sticking out from under the table. The North Boys leader just shook his head slowly, never taking his eyes off Bixby. The swagger vanished, along with the threatening expression on the lowlife's face. Wise move, Abbott thought. Another step closer and Zelly would have carved his name in the scumbag's chest – big style.

With a disgusted snarl, Bixby stalked back out of Ronnie's, the door slamming.

'Let's talk,' Abbott said.

'About what?'

'These rumours––'

'What rumours?' Zelly said, patting the air.

'Someone's eyeing up our territories.'

'Don't shit me.'

'It's just what I've heard.'

Zelly's eyes lit up at the mere mention of confrontation. 'I'm all for a fight.'

'We need to find out who's behind it first.'

'You must know something, you little prick. Who? Just give me a name.'

Abbott considered this, then changed tack. 'How come the filth is hassling everyone on both sides of the estate? What's going on?'

'What do you mean?'

'I reckon someone's got an eye on our territories, bruv.'

'That's some serious shit,' Zelly said, angrily.

'Yeah, I don't think it's the filth that's the problem. It's whoever's trying to muscle in on our territories.'

'Fuck fam. I knew something weren't right. I could see it. Now I know.' Zelly laughed, a short barking sound. 'Shit, it's almost good the filth is everywhere. Keeps whoever it is from making a move.'

Abbott smiled. Finally, the penny had dropped. He leaned over and tapped the table with a finger. 'We need to work together on this one, bruv. North Boys and Southside Gang as one. If not, we'll both be brown bread.'

Zelly nodded. 'You're right. I'll put my feelers out, see what the word on the street is. These bastards need to be taken down. . . and quick like.'

'I'll do the same,' Abbott agreed. 'Let's meet in twenty-four hours.'

A truce had been struck, but neither side seemed willing to yield ground for fear of repercussions. Nothing was straightforward anymore, and compromise was an ugly word on the Clapton Park Estate. Now the police had taken back control of the streets, everyone needed to dodge for cover.

Closing the coffee bar door behind him, Abbott reached for a cigarette to mask his uncertainty. It was then he noticed what looked to be an unmarked police van. It was parked up outside the corner shop. Uncertainty gripped him, and it wasn't looking good suddenly.

Had he been followed?

Desperate to reach home territory, his pace quickened. Much safer in numbers, he thought. And, if someone did have eyes on his patch, he would deal with it as only he knew how.

CHAPTER SIX

Jack Mason hated flawed journalism, and he was fuming. To blame racial hatred for the latest stabbing on the Clapton Park Estate was utterly ludicrous. The press were clutching at straws, manipulating the truth with the sole intention of increasing readership. Not only that, they were spreading racial tension and the community was up in arms over it. Serves them right, he thought. It was editorial vandalism gone mad.

Mason dropped the newspaper into his waste bin and turned his attention back to the crime board. There was no mistaking the level of violence used in the attack. Blood spatter everywhere, ceilings and walls, but very little in the way of hard evidence. Yes, they'd opened up a few fresh leads on the estate, but they'd been met by an unbreakable wall of silence. This was a desperately dangerous place to live, and these people who ruled it had different ways of getting to you. But that's how some hardened criminals would operate; spreading fear into a community and threatening reprisals if anyone stepped out of line.

Something was wrong; he knew it. An old man was dead, and apart from a few scraps of family gossip no one else was willing to talk.

God, what a mess!

Mason's morning had started badly. Close to Clapton Square, the rooftops of St John Mansions were blanketed in thick frost. The temperature had plummeted rapidly these past twenty-four hours and the forecast was for heavy snow. It wouldn't take much for the streets of Hackney to be gridlocked with abandoned vehicles. Typical, Mason thought. Anything that could go wrong, was going wrong.

Hands cupping a warm mug of black coffee, Mason cast a critical eye over the timeline and tried to take in the bigger picture. Apart from a few grainy images of potential candidates, nothing was clear cut. Not that he believed crime wasn't still being committed on the estate, it was, and that worried him. He knew from experience that two gangs controlled the Clapton Park Estate. One to the north, and one to the south. Though ASBOs abounded on both sides, it didn't seem to deter the gang leaders from continuing their campaign of fuelling violence in order to maintain a tight grip on their drug distribution networks. Dealers were everywhere. Behind the bowling alley, outside the newsagent's shops, and all along Rushmore Road. But attitudes were changing. Knives had arrived in the capital, along with baseball bats, cudgels, and sticks with nails on. The increase of heavier drugs coming down from Birmingham had certainly left its mark on the city, stopping it was the problem.

His thoughts returned back to the crime board. Truly, Mason was looking for inspiration and unsure where to find it.

'What about local pawn shops?' DCI Cummins said thoughtfully as he joined Mason in front of the crime board. 'Have we had any more feedback?'

'Not heard a dicky bird, Boss.'

'Pity. I was rather hoping someone would have pawned it by now. Find the watch, and it could open up Pandora's box. Whoever's responsible knows what they're doing. If not, they'd have moved it on by now.'

'That's if it hasn't already been melted down for its gold content, of course.'

'That would appear the safest option, but I'm not convinced that will happen.' Cummins turned to Mason and frowned. 'This was a professional job, and the person responsible knows how to deal with it.'

'An inside job, do you think?'

'Could be, and there's a strong hint of brinkmanship about the way they've gone about it.'

Mason looked at his boss oddly. 'Brinkmanship. What do you mean by that exactly?'

'See here,' Cummins said, tapping the crime board with the back of his hand. 'The way only some of the drawers have actually been rifled through?'

Mason peered at the photograph and nodded.

'A professional burglar – or one that didn't know exactly what he was looking for – would simply pull out all of them, tip out the contents and sift through for the good stuff.' Cummins pointed to the photographs of

Watkins' body. 'And here, these wounds. What did the coroner say again?'

Mason flipped back through the notes on the desk. 'Blunt force trauma to the head, broken ribs, severe bruising to the neck and back, and minor lacerations to his face and upper limbs.'

'Yeah, now, did the coroner say WHEN all these injuries took place?'

Mason frowned. 'Um, no...'

'Because I'd bet twenty quid the injuries to the ribs, back and neck occurred after the head injury.

'What do you mean?'

'The head wound was terminal. The lacerations clearly self-defence. The rest...'

'...Just a cover-up? Make it seem like hooligans?'

Cummins nodded. 'People are creatures of habit, they hide their worldly possessions in the most obvious of places.'

'Like under the floorboards, or stuffed behind furniture?'

'Think about it,' Cummins said. 'Where do you hide the things that *you* don't want people to find?'

'Umm–– I see what you're getting at.'

'This wasn't a gang of hooligans who turned old Harold Watkins' flat over. It was simply made to look that way.'

'Hence the brinkmanship?'

'Precisely.'

Uncanny, Mason thought. Where others struggled to find answers, Cummins was logically working his way through the crime scene as if it were a worksheet. He was good, extremely good.

Mason drained his second coffee of the morning and picked up a bundle of case files he'd dropped on his desk earlier.

'The problem we're faced with is we don't have a checklist of what was stolen, and there's no record of insurance cover being taken out either. According to neighbours, the old man lived a quiet, unassuming life and seldom left his premises.'

'A professional criminal would have known that too,' Cummins said.

'They could have,' Mason agreed, 'but I'm buggered if I can find a connection.'

The Chief Inspector turned to face him again. 'It's a well-known fact that old people hoard cash in their property, as they're far less mobile and can't get to the banks as often as they would like. I remember my mother doing it. God bless her. She kept her money hidden in a biscuit tin at the bottom of the pantry.' Cummins tapped the crime board with the back of his hand again. 'The question we should be asking ourselves is, did he plan to kill the old man or was he just intending to scare him off?'

'That puts a different slant on it, of course.'

'Indeed.' Cummins took a step back from the crime board, thinking. 'We need to find the murder weapon, as it will tell us a lot more about him.'

'If only,' Mason shrugged.

Cummins laughed out loud. 'Follow your instincts, Sergeant. Yes, there could be a connection to local gangs here, but I doubt it. Our suspect is keeping a low profile, it's a matter of weeding him out.'

'A local man?' Mason suggested.

'If not, they know someone who is.'

'An informant perhaps?'

'Could be. It's beginning to look more like an inside job to me.' Cummins scratched the side of his head in thought. 'What about this Tony guy who threatened you at knifepoint? He could be pivotal in all of this. If we can link him to the crime scene around the time of the attack, it could be the breakthrough we're looking for.'

'I'm working on it.'

'Good man. Let's bring him in for questioning. He's bound to know something.'

Mason could almost hear the cogs ticking away inside the chief inspector's head. It was good watching him work, and he was learning a lot.

'What about the stolen watch?'

'It's still our best lead, so you'll need to keep an eye out for it. People talk. They make things happen when you least expect them to.'

'Maybe I should put my feelers out.'

'Tread carefully, Sergeant. I know this area as well as you do. Informants can quickly bleed you dry for little or no reward.' Cummins smiled. 'The one golden rule I've learnt over the years is, moles can work against you by selling your information on for a higher price.'

'I'll bear that in mind, Boss.' Mason nodded, already thinking about future plans.

'Let's see what this latest clampdown throws up. Gang leaders aren't daft. The minute we loosen our grip on the estate they'll be keen to move back into it again. When they do, we'll slip a couple of undercover operators into the area and find out what's going on.'

Mason jotted a few notes down.

'What about other known felons in the area?'

'Do not assume anything in this game. Whoever carried out this atrocity will be watching us like a hawk. That's how these people operate, behind uncertainty.' Cummins smiled. 'I know this is your first major assignment and you're keen to impress. Nothing wrong with that, of course. I did the same myself when I took charge of my first small team of detectives. If you want some advice, take a step back and try not to rush into things.'

'I'll find the person responsible. I give you my solemn word on that.'

'I'm sure you will.'

Mason held Cummins gaze. 'Thanks for the advice, I appreciate it.'

'Look, listen, and learn,' Cummins said, tapping his head with a forefinger. 'For what it's worth, I would concentrate my efforts on the outlying estates. When residents are refusing to talk, it usually means that someone is intimidating them. The trick is, to find out who.'

Nodding his thanks, Mason felt sure he was on track.

CHAPTER
SEVEN

There were no children playing on the streets of Tower Hamlets that afternoon, the only sound was police sirens passing. Busy times, Mason thought, as he turned his collar up against the rain and made towards the subway dubbed "Murder Alley." Known as a RED SCORE on the Metropolitan Police crime matrix, this rundown part of the estate was a breeding ground for some of London's most notorious felons. Driven by gangs with an increasing desire to profit from major crime, the only prospect for many low life offenders was to climb up the criminal ladder. Mason understood their mentality and their desires. Life was a bitch, and unless you fought your way out of the poverty trap it was easy to fall through the cracks.

Not all residents were bad. There were a number of law-abiding citizens amongst the trash who terrorised the estate, but they were few and far between. Knife crime ran rife here, and shootings were an all too regular occurrence. What the area needed was a release valve according to local pastor Claudette McDonald. Something to stem the violence. The issue was, she'd buried more of her flock through violent street related gang wars than she dared to admit. Mason felt sorry for her, and thought she was fighting a losing battle.

'My only suggestion is to speak to Peter Daniels,' the pastor said, sipping her tea.

'Daniels? God's Messenger?'

Pastor McDonald grimaced. 'I'd rather we didn't use that nickname, please, Detective Mason. But yes, having recently found God, Peter is doing remarkable work in the community.'

'So, he's a reformed man?'

The pastor's response was hesitant and drawn out.

'I take it you know Peter?'

'The last I heard he'd been released from Wormwood Scrubs after serving a three-year prison sentence for handling stolen property.'

'Yes, I did hear something about that.'

'So, how did you and Peter meet?' asked Mason.

'He came via a friend. It's amazing really. . . how much a person can change given the right opportunity.' The pastor held eye contact. 'Peter has done an awful lot of good work in the community, especially here at the church.'

'Is he a regular attender?'

Pastor McDonald spread her hands expansively and laughed. 'Peter is more a community man, he helps me out from time to time with the more difficult problems.'

Mason smiled inwardly. Peter Daniels was known for two things: a knack for violence and making a living in shifting high-end goods for the East End underworld.

Something didn't sit right, and he would need to tread carefully.

Mason put his cup down as he stood to leave.

'You've been most helpful, and I can't thank you enough.'

'It's been a pleasure meeting you Detective Sergeant,' Pastor McDonald replied.

He left through the vestry door.

***

Hands in pockets, eyes peeled and fixed straight ahead, Mason decided against visiting the Greasy Spoon. Not today at least. It was far too risky; if the local Mafiosi caught him sniffing around one of their local pubs, he'd be in for a hiding to nothing. It was all about infiltrating the criminal underworld – talking to the people in the know. He knew Peter Daniels from old. The man was an out-and-out con man who liked the smell of money and would do anything to get his hands on it. Strange, Mason thought, what was Daniels up to with the church?

It had stopped raining when he finally reached his destination – a redbrick tenement flat with a large entrance hall and wood panel flooring. No 24 was on the second floor. An end flat, along a dimly lit corridor and overlooking a vandalised children's play area.

He rang the doorbell and heard movement from within.

Seconds later, the door opened, and a short, thin man in his late thirties appeared wearing football shorts, a green T-shirt, and sneakers. He was carrying a wine bottle in his hand and had trouble written all over his face.

'What do you want?' he asked, in an aggressive reedy voice.

'I'm looking for God's Messenger,' Mason said. 'Do you happen to know where I can find such a man?'

'You police?'

'No. What makes you think I am?'

'Cos the last time those bastards paid me a visit they smashed my frigging door down.' Daniels looked quizzically across at Mason. 'They found nowt, but they still turned the place over.'

Mason feigned displeasure. 'Sorry to hear.'

'I'm no angel. I just happen to live on an estate full of arseholes.'

'Any chance I can come in?'

'Not until I know who you are.'

'A colleague of yours sent me. He thinks you can help.'

Daniels looked him up and down, then beckoned him inside.

The living room was small, cramped, and not as Mason had expected to find it. Daylight poured in through the tilted window blinds, and airborne dust particles floated in a room that stank of stale cigarette smoke.

'What's on your mind?' Daniels asked, turning sharply to confront him.

'I'm looking for information.'

'What kind?'

The man oozed confidence, bags of it, and obviously knew how to handle himself.

'A few days ago, my mate's fathers flat was turned over and I'm not sleeping at all well thinking about it.'

'Your friend's father's flat?' Daniels shrugged, turning back towards what Mason assumed was the cramped kitchen.

'Yeah. That's right.'

'What's that got to do with me?'

Mason inhaled deeply. He'd never grown tired of rogues' posturing; never got bored. What he was really after was hard evidence – and Watkins' stolen watch was as good a starting place as any.

The sergeant never took his eyes off Daniels. 'Whoever broke into my friend's father's flat, stole a number of valuable items.'

'Like what?'

'I'm particularly interested in a gold watch.'

'And?'

Mason managed a thin watery smile. 'There's a part of me says that it might be melted down for its scrap value, and I don't want that to happen.'

'What makes you think I can help?'

Mason trod cautiously. 'Your colleague told me to contact you.'

'Does he have a name?'

'I'd rather not say.'

Daniels eyed him with suspicion. 'What kind of watch are we talking about here?'

'It's a Vacheron Constantin Geneve. It has a round gold face with Roman numerals and an extra-flat mechanical hand winding mechanism.'

'That's an expensive piece of kit.'

'Is it?' Mason shrugged.

Daniels first looked puzzled, then affronted. 'When did you say this watch was nicked?'

'A few days ago, over on the Clapton Park Estate.'

'And what makes you think I can help you?' Daniels repeated firmly.

Mason drew back knowing full well he was moving into dangerous territory. One fraudulent slip of the tongue, a mis-timed answer, and he could end up facing the wrath of a hardened criminal. He stood for a moment, motionless, Daniels' dark inquisitive eyes bearing down at him.

'I'm willing to pay good money.'

The mere mention of money and Daniels' eyes lit up. 'Yeah. But I don't think you've told me everything about your friend's father's flat.'

'What is it you want to know?'

'This isn't the old man who was freeze-framed over on Ambergate Court, by any chance?'

'It could be––'

'If it is, you're talking to the wrong person.'

'Why, is there a problem?'

Daniels chose his next words carefully. 'What makes you think I'd want to get mixed up in a murder?'

'All I'm asking for is the watch back.'

'It's not that easy. . . lots of people will be looking out for it.'

'Like whom?'

'You'd be surprised.' Daniels' tone was aggressive. 'Was he a relative of yours?'

'No. Just a good friend.'

'So, what's your interest in this watch?'

Mason felt the knot in his stomach tighten. Daniels was asking all the wrong questions, and that worried him. It was time to change tack, before his cover was blown.

'Can you get it back?'

'I probably can. But that ain't free.'

Mason tried to hide his excitement. He swallowed hard and nodded. 'I've heard nothing big happens around here without you at least knowing about it.'

Daniels shrugged. Clearly, he wasn't going to give much else away. 'Five hundred now. Five hundred when I find it.'

'That's an awful lot of money.'

'Take it or leave it. You want a watch, I can find the watch. It's gonna cost you a grand.'

Mason tried to conceal his irritation at Daniels' condescending tone. Now wasn't the time for negotiation. He held out a hand and Daniels shook it. An agreement had been struck, and it was unlikely his informant would renege on the deal. Mason's biggest concern, if he could think of one, was that moles had a habit of sniffing the wrong kind of information out. Looking for Watkins' watch was one thing, but if Daniels ever discovered he'd unwittingly been tricked into working for an undercover police officer – what then?

Mason reached into his back pocket and pulled out a roll of marked bank notes.

'Five hundred now, and five hundred when I get the watch back,' he sighed.

Daniels' eyes narrowed. 'Give me a couple of days. I'll see what I can do.'

'Nice doing business with you,' Mason said, shaking Daniels' oversized, calloused hand again.

Mason wrote his details down on a slip of paper and handed it to Daniels. This was a dangerous place to be caught out in, and he was relieved to leave by the back door.

***

It had stopped raining when Mason reached the pre-arranged pick up point. Just out of habit he checked his surroundings before sliding into the passenger seat of the unmarked Vauxhall Corsa. He'd been working far too much overtime lately and it was beginning to catch up on him. Brenda was right, burning the candle at both ends was asking for serious trouble. He was worn out, exhausted as if entering into a cul-de-sac on a dark windswept night. He would need to slow down, ease back on the work throttle. If that was humanly possible.

Constable Summers peered at him from the driver's seat and said. 'Any luck?'

'He took the bait, if that's what you mean.'

'What about the watch?'

'I'm confident he'll point us in the right direction.'

'Big fish in little ponds are usually dangerous predators, Sarge. But if anyone knows its whereabouts, it's Peter Daniels.'

'Let's hope you're right, cos I've just handed him five hundred quid of hard-earned police funds to get it back.'

'I hope you made him sign for it,' Summers grinned.

'Sod off.'

Seconds later they joined the steady flow of traffic heading west towards Hackney South. More than pleased with his arrangements, Mason was confident they were making steady progress at last. If Daniels did lead them to the watch's whereabouts, it would make life a lot easier. In his mind were two possible scenarios. If the watch hadn't been moved on or melted down, it still had to be in the killer's possession. And, if local gangs weren't involved in the old man's murder, then who else was in the frame? Thinking about this, he opened his notebook and began to jot a few things down. It was then he remembered what DCI Cummins had told him about informants selling your information on to the highest bidder.

Too late for that now, he groaned.

Hopefully Daniels would come up trumps.

CHAPTER EIGHT

Jack Mason was sitting at the kitchen table, watching breakfast television and slowly drinking his second cup of coffee. Brenda was fast asleep in bed. Not wishing to disturb her, he'd showered, then dressed in the back bedroom. The heavy snowfall that had been forecast earlier still hadn't materialised. It was heading north according to the weather experts, towards the Midlands and away from the capital.

It was Wednesday, and Brenda was meeting with friends that morning – after she'd finished her aqua natal yoga class. Sometimes he wondered what all the fuss was about, as his wife detested swimming at the best of times. With only a few weeks to go before the baby was due, she swore it was nurturing her self-confidence.

Meanwhile, for him, these past few weeks had been a living hell. He'd been working far too much overtime lately and not enough time spent at home. Brenda felt isolated, lonely, and he couldn't say that he blamed her. He'd been a fool to think his workload would ease off whilst a killer was still on the loose.

'One day,' the sergeant muttered.

The drive to Clapton Park took a little over fifty minutes, with long tailbacks until reaching Rushmore Road. On entering the estate, the car was stopped by a smug-faced constable intent on making his presence felt. Security was tight, it had to be, as this was a full-on murder enquiry.

'Anymore trouble from local youths?' Mason asked, as he slowed to stop, flashing his warrant card.

'No, Sarge,' the constable replied. 'It's been relatively quiet these past few days.'

'Good man.'

Mason climbed out of the unmarked BMW pool car and habitually checked his watch. Now thinking along the lines of DCI Cummins, there was every chance the killer was local. Most police officers he knew worked on their instincts. It was a copper's nose – akin to a trained drugs dog sniffing out narcotics in a crowded airport. One thing was for sure, no matter how many criminals were taken off the streets during an investigation, there were plenty of others to step into their shoes. Some occupations were never short of recruits, and being a criminal was one of them.

On reaching the tenth floor, Mason tried to get his head around it all. How someone could callously bludgeon a frail old pensioner to death beggared belief. Above all else, Mason hated those who picked on the old and vulnerable as there was no real recovery from the physical and mental cruelty it caused. This case was slightly different, though, and had changed his thoughts on the way people reacted when put under pressure.

Whoever the killer was, he'd instilled so much fear into the estate that no one was willing to say anything, let alone be seen with them.

It was a sad state of affairs, and Mason had never wavered in his abhorrence towards the killer's lack of empathy.

Who would be next?

The living room was small, with commanding views overlooking the west bank of the Hackney Cut and the River Lee. To his right lay Stratford and West Ham Park, further afield the county boroughs of East Ham and Barking. Not that he would ever choose to live here but the outlook was absolutely stunning.

Mason swivelled on his heels the moment he heard the hallway door being pushed open.

'Detective Sergeant Mason?' the visitor said. 'George Coleman... forensics.'

They'd never met before, but Mason was aware of Coleman's thoroughness in investigating a crime scene. Bald except for a few grey chevrons above the ears, he had a thin, gaunt face, and wore thick, horn-rimmed spectacles now perched on the top of his head. Dressed more for comfort than appearance, Coleman's mud-spattered shoes told him this wasn't the officer's only port of call that morning. These were busy times, and everyone was having to work flat out in an effort to close out leads.

'Pleased to finally catch up with you, George,' Mason said, extending out a hand.

'This isn't your first visit to the flat, I take it?'

'No,' Mason explained. 'I'm going back over old ground in case I've missed out on something.'

'Same here, you can never be too thorough,' Coleman agreed. The forensic officer stared at his clipboard and frowned. 'Is there anything I can help you with before I make a start?'

'There is one thing,' Mason said, thoughtfully. 'You can walk me through what actually took place here.'

'Yes, of course.' Coleman gestured towards the open doorway. 'According to the post-mortem report, the victim suffered blunt force trauma to the head. This was a particularly nasty assault, and the poor bugger didn't stand a chance.'

'Pre-meditated do you think?'

'Nothing else fits the frame. We still have a lot of lab work to get through, which could throw more light on the situation, of course.'

Mason nodded as he took down some notes. A confident officer by the sounds, Coleman was walking him through a set sequence of events he already knew. He watched as the forensic officer's eyes narrowed a fraction and sensed an underlying resentment in his voice. This type of crime was never easy, and police officers who attended them were always left with the niggling doubt the perpetrator might walk free from it all. It was all about tying up loose ends, making sure you'd covered every eventuality.

'It's a pity we still haven't recovered the murder weapon,' Mason said.

'Yes. Whatever he used to attack his victim with he used it with considerable force. By all accounts, it's a blessing in disguise the old man never recovered, as bone fragments had seemingly punctured his brain and would have left him in a vegetative state for the rest of his days.'

Mason winced. 'Nasty. What's your take on it exactly?'

'Harold Watkins was initially found slumped unconscious beneath the lounge window.' Coleman gestured towards a heavily blood-stained rug. 'According to the police doctor in attendance, he was struck several massive blows to the left side of his skull in what is described as an escalated attack.'

'Any indications as to how long it lasted?'

'Hard to say.' Coleman paused in thought before pointing to blood spatter running across one of the interior walls. 'The force of the blows caused irreparable damage to the cerebellum which had obviously rendered him unconscious at some point. But looking at the injuries, it's my view this wasn't a prolonged attack.'

'If he was found beneath the window, could he have been dragged there at some later point?'

'No. There's nothing to suggest the body was ever moved.'

Mason raised his eyebrows. 'And we know he didn't put up much of a fight?'

'The evidence points to that. From the angle of the body blows the victim was trying to move away from his attacker rather than resist. We know the assailant is left-handed from the angle of the wounds. Which narrows it down considerably.'

'I've been thinking about that,' Mason added.

Coleman smiled. 'He could be ambidextrous, of course.'

As far as Mason could remember, the injuries outlined in the post-mortem report were consistent with what Coleman had been telling him. Dr James Penny, the Home Office Pathologist, had reported multiple fractures to the left side of the skull, and seven heavy bruise marks to the upper body. Two to the left side of the head, two to the left shoulder, and three to the upper torso. But of everything, it was the sheer level of destruction to the property that concerned Mason most. Upturned furniture, broken ornaments strewn about the floor, and clothes scattered around like confetti. It felt like the aftermath of a previous case he'd once worked on.

'Strange, no fingerprints. . .' Mason said, thoughtfully.

'He wore surgical gloves, which meant he came prepared.'

'What else did you find?'

'We managed to recover minute traces of soil sample from the living room carpet. It's consistent with samples found along the Lee Navigation.'

'Brought here by the victim?' Mason suggested.

Coleman hesitated. 'We found no traces of it on any of the victim's footwear.'

'That is interesting. The suspect perhaps?'

'Possible. Though one of the neighbours could have brought it here.'

Mason made a note of it then pocketed his notebook. Why on earth hadn't they picked up on that before? He knew it was a gradual process...but still. Even so, things were about to change and a new era of forensics was being ushered in, and once in custody, DNA samples were being taken from potential suspects and placed on a National Data register. The future looked bright, and it couldn't come fast enough as far as Mason was concerned.

As his eyes toured the room, the sergeant noticed a distinct lack of valuables on show. Information was a detective's lifeblood. It came in many guises: interviews, criminal records, informants, newspaper reports, and could often be found tucked away in coroners' reports. No, Mason thought. Everything that could be done was being done. Something would surface, and usually did. If it wasn't local gossip that caught the murderer out it would be something they'd stolen and tried to move on.

Hands in pockets, Mason stared out of the tenth-floor window and pondered his options. He'd need to be patient, bide his time in the hope the killer would make a mistake. Had they missed something; a vital piece of evidence, or was someone not telling them the truth? They were on the right track, he was certain of that, but nothing jumped out at him at the moment.

He turned sharply.

'Thank you, George. At least I now have a clearer picture of what actually took place here.'

'Glad to help.'

Mason grimaced. 'These soil samples you recently uncovered. Perhaps we should take a closer look. If our suspect approached the crime scene from the direction of the Lee Navigation it could put a whole new slant on things.'

Coleman nodded. 'I'd check along the riverbank if I were you. Stay within a five-mile radius of the nearest point from here, and you'll not go wrong. It might also be worth talking to the narrowboat community. . . find out what they have to say.'

'Sounds like a plan.'

Coleman made a little sweeping gesture. 'When I'm finished here, I'll fax you a copy of my report. You never know, it might throw up a few fresh leads.'

Mason nodded his appreciation.

'Thanks again. That would be extremely useful.'

CHAPTER NINE

There was something about The Buzzcocks that suited the atmosphere perfectly. The louder the better, Tony Abbott thought. It was 8.30 am and, apart from a couple of pensioners drinking coffee, Ronnie's Coffee Bar was empty. He needed something to stimulate his adrenal glands, and "Harmony in My Head" was perfect. Deep down, Abbott wasn't sure how his meeting with Zelly would pan out. Now the police had surprisingly eased their stranglehold on the estate, he was keen to break ties with the North Boys. There were deals to be struck, old scores to settle, and he was itching to get moving.

Abbott scooted a seat up opposite Zelly and hunched his shoulders. But that wasn't all – something odd had caught his attention that morning and it caused him to burst out laughing.

'What's with the bright orange shades, bruv.'

The North Boys' leader drew back in his seat unimpressed. 'Don't shit me. What have you heard?'

'The old bill is moving out.'

Zelly's face twitched. 'And?'

'We're both in the clear, bruv.'

Zelly poked a threatening finger at Abbott. A defiant gesture. Intimidating. Neither gang leader was willing to give ground and they we're heading for an all-out confrontation.

'For now, but the mother fucks will be back.'

'What have you heard?'

Zelly gave Abbott a toxic look. 'They're still hanging around Ambergate Court.'

'Don't crap me.'

'Yeah. And they're looking for something.'

Abbott tried to conceal his frustration at Zelly's tone. 'Not heard that. What are they looking for?'

'I dunno.'

Abbott shot Zelly a daggers' look. 'Why be bringing it up if you ain't heard something?'

'Cos.'

'Cos, what?'

'I heard a shit-load of valuables were nicked from the old man's flat, and they want them back.'

'Like what?'

'How the fuck would I know,' Zelly said, angrily. 'I wasn't there!'

Abbott was about to say something but quickly thought better of it. Zelly's demeanour had changed, as if the fuse had been lit. But Zelly wasn't smart, and his look was confused, as if grappling to kick his dumb brain into gear.

'What now, bruv?'

'Biz as usual, eh?'

'So, our deal's off?'

Zelly pushed back in his seat. 'What do you think, motherfucker?'

It was then Abbott realised that his back was to the door and Zelly wasn't alone anymore. There were others, and they were spoiling for a fight. Abbott gripped the tubular metal armrests of his chair and felt the sides flex. It wasn't the best environment to be caught out in, not without a knife. Deep down he actually felt sorry for the North Boys' leader. If the man had half a brain, he'd be dangerous.

Abbott stood to leave.

'Stay cool, bruv.'

'Fuck you.'

Well, what did Zelly expect? In truth, Abbott had always fancied his chances as the kingpin of the estate, it was the driving force behind every decision he made. There was big money to be had, girls, power, and everyone looked up to you. Sure, two of his boys had got merked, stuck by knives over street corners. But that was the risk you took. And the rewards ... the rewards were everything.

Abbott beat a hasty retreat from Ronnie's Coffee Shop and braced himself for the inevitable. The streets were a dangerous place once again, and anything was fair game! The moment he stepped into the newsagent's shop and saw the headlines and froze.

POLICE CLOSE TO ARRESTING HAROLD WATKINS KILLER.

'Holy shit,' Abbott gasped.

Something dark stirred in the pit of the Southside Gang leader's stomach, and not for the first time he felt vulnerable that morning. Shit happened, but this was real bad stuff. News didn't normally matter to Tony. Old white dicks writing about shit they didn't know or understand, and not giving a toss about what was really going down on the streets.

Unsure of his next move, Abbott tucked the newspaper inside his shirt and made a quick dash for the newsagent's door. He wasn't daft and knew that press junk-it were always out to make money. That's what paid the bills. Even so, this news was pure dynamite and whoever had printed it had got their information from somewhere.

But where? And who was feeding them this crap?

For a start, if the filth did have a dodgy dealer in mind, then surely, they'd have pulled them before now. And another thing, why flood the estate with Met muscle? None of it made sense. He knew big brother was completely ineffective against gangs and had been so ever since the Misuse of Drugs Act. The idea the police were protecting its citizens from street crime was utter bollocks. Then again, he reasoned. Show signs of weakness and the chasing pack would rip you apart as soon as look at you.

Abbott hunched his shoulders in an aggressive stance as he slipped into the street in a hurry. He couldn't entirely ignore the fact the North Boys may have stitched him up – like the moment they'd tried to turn him over in

Ronnie's. Threats didn't get much clearer than that, and this was serious stuff.

His phone rang, and he answered it.

'What!'

'The filth is back.'

'No shit?'

'Defo. You gotta believe me.'

'Where?'

'Southside is crawling with them.'

Abbott ended the call and stood for a moment, thinking. The only option left to him was to warn his dealer network to keep a low profile. Bad news spread like wildfire but good news went unreported. The police were crafty bastards, and sooner than later they'd come knocking on everyone's door – and they were good at that.

What to do next?

CHAPTER
TEN

The High Street had altered very little, it was just as Jack Mason remembered it. The barber shop had gone, along with the local tobacconist which was now a fruit and veg shop with a brightly coloured facade. One thing that hadn't changed over the years was Tommy Robinson's betting shop, full of disillusioned punters dreaming of utopia. The funny thing was Mason recalled the day it burnt down.

It had been a Tuesday afternoon, and he'd been walking home from school. The first thing he'd noticed was the smoke, billowing out of the roof, spreading in all directions. By the time he'd reached the betting shop, it was completely ablaze. He had stood well back, watching the firefighters wrestle with the flames. Although nobody was injured, it took them three hours to finally bring the blaze under control, by which time the building was well and truly gutted.

It was the talk of the estate, and rumours ran rife that one of the cashiers had pocketed the entire weekly takings after setting fire to a storeroom. He thought he'd got away with it, but he hadn't, of course. When the police raided the cashier's house and found ten thousand pounds stuffed under his daughter's mattress, he couldn't explain how it had got there. It was strange what some people thought they could get away with, and arson was a common crime to commit in an attempt to destroy evidence.

Blinking away the memories, Mason stepped up to the busy post office counter, flashed his warrant card through the protection screen and made himself known.

'Hello, Jack,' the friendly female cashier smiled. 'Long time no see. What brings you to this neck of the woods?'

Not a tall woman, petite with short blonde hair, Janet Jute had worked at the post office for as long as Mason could remember. He knew her brother, a drayman who'd worked at the local brewery. But that was a few years ago; he was suffering from Parkinson's disease now and didn't have long to live.

'Official business, I'm afraid,' Mason replied.

'How can we help?'

'There's been reports that an unlawful cash withdrawal was made from your cash machine.' Mason smiled as he pocketed his warrant card. 'I'm here to follow it up.'

She looked at him oddly. 'What time was this?'

'Last night. It was flagged up on the bank's stolen card register.' Mason frowned, thinking about the ramifications of this. 'I've had a look at your machine, and it doesn't appear to have been tampered with.'

She hesitated. 'How much was taken?'

Mason skipped the question. 'What security arrangements do you have in place?'

'The premises are burglar alarmed and there's CCTV covering the front of the building, if that's what you're looking for.'

Mason leaned in closer. 'I need to take a look at last night's CCTV footage.'

Jute pursed her lips and nodded. 'Give me a few minutes, and I'll sort something out for you.'

'Splendid,' Mason nodded.

She peered at him with suspicion before ducking under the counter. 'I presume you'll want the original tape?'

'We do, and we'll return it as soon as we're finished.'

'It's not the best system in the world. I've reported it to head office on numerous occasions but nothing ever gets done about it.'

Not wanting to get involved in internal politics, or small talk, Mason remained tight-lipped. Whoever had made a cash withdrawal, wasn't a million miles from Harold Watkins' flat. But there lay another problem, as experienced criminals were devious sods and usually got someone else to do their dirty work for them.

'Will that be all?' said Jute, handing Mason the cassette.

'Yes, for now. Thank you.'

She looked at him pensively. 'Like I say, I wouldn't pin my hopes on it if I were you. That said, it might give you an indication as to what's been going on around here lately.'

'This isn't the first time, then?'

'You'd be surprised, Jack.'

'Really?'

'Yes. It happens regularly once we shut up shop. In the last fortnight alone, we've removed at least two trapping devices from the machine that I'm aware of.'

Mason cocked his head to one side. 'Trapping devices. What's that all about?'

'It's a device they fit to the card slot which prevents it from being returned. Nothing sophisticated, but once you've left the area, they simply prise your card back out of the slot along with your card entry details.'

'Christ,' Mason groaned. 'Is there no end to what these people get up to?'

'I'm afraid not.' She picked up a pile of envelopes, then put them down again. 'Yours isn't the only bank account that's been tampered with in the last three months. We've dealt with dozens of them.'

Mason stared at her in disbelief. 'It doesn't sound good.'

'It's not. But now that you know, perhaps you could give us some assistance.'

'Leave it with me.'

He signed for the cassette and left into bright sunshine. It wasn't all bad news then; his hunch had paid dividends and he had a new line of enquiries to investigate.

***

Now onto his third cup of coffee, Mason stared at the small team of police officers huddled around the monitor screen. Janet Jute was right: it wasn't the best CCTV footage. The images were grainy, blurred, but at least they were making progress.

From what he could see, the suspect was wearing a black hoodie pulled low over his head and obscuring his face from view. Not a muscular man by appearance, around six foot-two with long skinny legs and big feet, it wasn't a lot to go at. But sometimes you got lucky and a culprit's name sprang out at you. Not this time, though. Whoever had made the withdrawal from the post office cash machine knew how to avoid detection.

Despite their setbacks, after lunch, they pored over the Police National Database again. The PND, as it was better known, was a very effective tool in their armoury and could save them an awful lot of leg work at times. Not only did it allow all UK police forces to share intelligence, it prevented serious organised crime from escalating out of control and kept the real serial offenders from committing further offences. Mason loved it and couldn't stop singing his praises about it. It did have its low points, but the benefits far outweighed the risks as far as the sergeant was concerned.

After an hour spent trying to pick their way through dozens of grainy images, they were joined by the chief inspector. Smartly turned out in a brown three-piece suit, Cummins was a snappy dresser. Visual image played an important part in his everyday appearance, it seemed. Nothing wrong with that. If anything, it sent out a strong message that you were dealing with a professional at the top of his game. Mason made a mental note of it.

It was Friday, and with the weekend looming ever closer, there was always the possibility of having to stay late and finish the job. Not that Mason would ever complain, but after a long arduous week chasing shadows, he was looking forward to some quality home time with Brenda.

Cummins linked his hands behind his neck as he listened to Mason's explanations. His face more serious than usual, he kept shaking his head as if irritated by something. Not one for giving much away, the Chief Inspector finally leaned over and pointed to the computer screen.

'Can we sharpen the image?'

'That's the best I can do,' PC Sheila White replied.

'Blimey, no wonder you're struggling. Let's rewind to the previous user.'

'What are we looking for?' asked DC Chambers, now in charge of the door-to-door enquiries.

Cummins digested the new information for several moments and then instructed White to forward the tape to its original position. 'Hold it right there,' the Chief Inspector suddenly exclaimed. 'Notice the way he picks the credit card out of the cash machine after he's completed the transaction – our suspect's naturally lefthanded.'

'You're right,' Mason nodded.

'And we know our killer's lefthanded,' added Chambers.

'Yes, but that doesn't mean it's our man. What it does tell us, though, is he's testing to see if the card is still active. Had he not been, he would have withdrawn a lot more cash than fifty quid.'

'Why doesn't he clear the whole account out?' asked White.

Cummins smiled. 'The bank will have a limit as to the amount of cash that can be withdrawn at any one given time. The suspect will know that too, so by taking out small amounts at a time he'll not flag suspicion with the banks.'

'The crafty sod,' White laughed. 'But how the hell did he get hold of the old man's card details in the first place?'

As White's long slender fingers danced over the keyboard like a pianist in concert, Mason explained. 'The PIN was probably skimmed at some point, which all adds to the attack being planned.'

'Cunning sods.'

Cummins puffed his cheeks out in thought. 'We need to expand our enquiries over on the Clapton Park estate. Grab a few suspect screenshots and get uniforms involved. If he is local, there's a good chance he'll be known to us – digging him out's the problem. In the meantime, let's see what other surveillance cameras we have at our disposal. It's my view he's not the killer, but he may be in contact with someone who is.' The Chief Inspector did a little jig-like dance as he pointed to the computer screen again. 'How did he get hold of Watkins' bank card? Who gave it to him? We need a clear picture of the suspect's known movements – his favourite haunts, who he meets, and what he gets up to after dark.'

'If he is local, he'll obviously be watching our movements,' Mason replied.

Cummins acknowledged with a nod. 'Any more news on the stolen watch?' he asked.

'No. Nothing,' lamented DC Summers, who had sat quietly throughout.

'I thought as much. What about your informant over in Tower Hamlets?' Cummins said, turning to face Mason. 'Has he said anything to you yet?'

Mason's face dropped. 'No.'

'Watkins' watch is obviously too hot to handle at the moment. We need to be patient, keep our ears to the ground and wait for it to surface again.'

'What about future cash withdrawals?' asked Chambers. 'When will he make the big hit, do you think?'

'He'll not do that until he's confident the bank hasn't cottoned on to him,' Cummins pointed a finger at the crime board. 'Which reminds me. We need to contact Watkins' bank about future cash withdrawals. The first hint of any movement we need to be on it like a flash.'

'What are the chances of him using the same cash machine again?' asked White.

Mason leaned over. 'Slim, I reckon. It's far too risky.'

'I agree,' Summers nodded.

Cummins was quiet for a moment as he flipped through the pages of his notebook. The DCI was still in good spirits, as well as he might have been. His wife, Jennifer, had just had a tickle on the bingo, the first in a long time according to him. Nine-hundred and fifty quid wasn't a huge sum of money, but it wasn't to be sniffed at either. It could have been more had she not shared with a friend. But beggars couldn't be choosers, not with that kind of windfall.

'The missing murder weapon,' said Cummins, looking up from his notebook. 'Do we have anymore feedback from forensics?'

'Nothing yet,' the sergeant replied. 'From what I gather, forensics believe the suspect went armed and took the murder weapon away with him when he left the victim's flat.'

'What makes them think the old man didn't keep it hidden behind his door?'

'He may well have done, but there's strong evidence to support that he went armed.'

Cummins raised his eyebrows. 'Even if he did, we need to cover every eventuality.'

Mason acknowledged with a nod but said nothing.

'Okay. There's plenty to be getting on with,' the Chief Inspector said, as he arched his back in thought. 'We need to think positively – watch, murder weapon, and witness accounts. Not necessarily in that order, but those are the major points of interest. In the meantime, I'll talk to the Superintendent about getting some additional resources.'

As the meeting began to break up, Mason's desk phone rang.

'Anything I should know?' Cummins frowned.

'It's the wife, Boss. She's spotted a 4-wheel travel system in Mothercare and is asking for advice on the colour.'

'When is the baby due?'

'In a couple of weeks.'

'Let's hope we catch our suspect before the sleepless nights kick in.'

'Chance would be a fine thing.'

'Yes. I fear you are right.'

Mason looked up from his desk feeling somewhat deflated. He hadn't had a good night's sleep in weeks, and it was slowly getting to him. Look on the positive side, he thought. In a fortnight from now there will be two beautiful women to contend with – and a killer behind bars.

CHAPTER
ELEVEN

Earlier that morning, Jack Mason had received confirmation that some numpty had made another cash withdrawal from Harold Watkins' bank account. The news had left him struggling to curb his emotions, and he was furious. He hated some crimes, particularly this one, and he'd made it a personal crusade to catch the culprit red-handed.

He was still deep in thought, when Bob Cummins approached him in the corridor. The Chief Inspector was carrying a large bundle of case files tucked under his arm. 'Ah, the very man. Do you have a second?'

'Certainly, Boss.'

'It's about the Watkins murder case.'

'What about it?'

'I've been thinking about the victim's flat. If the killer was known to Watkins, I find it rather incredulous we haven't been able to obtain a DNA match.'

'He may not have a criminal record.'

'It's possible, but if this was a planned attack, he's no beginner.' Cummins rearranged the files in his arms. 'Just on the off chance we've overlooked some vital piece of evidence, I've instructed forensics to take another look at the soil samples found in the victim's carpet. I'm curious as to what the connection is with the Lee Navigation.'

'I've been giving that some thought, Boss. There's every chance our suspect lives on the west side of the river, as it's more densely populated.'

'What if he works on the navigation itself, or owns a narrowboat?'

Mason pondered Cummins' statement for a moment. 'It's possible, but highly unlikely, don't you think?'

'Not really. Something's not right. We need to get a team down there, find out what's really going on. Let's start with the narrowboat community. While life on a canal boat can be idyllic for much of the year, winters are a different challenge. People don't move around as much during a cold snap and normally stay static. It could be something or nothing, but I've got a really good feeling about this.'

'I'll see to it, Boss.'

'Anything come of the post office video footage we looked at the other day?'

'It's strange you should ask, as I'm about to head over to Kingsland.'

'Kingsland?'

'We've received reports of another cash withdrawal from Watkins' bank account.'

'Really? It's not the same machine by any chance?' asked Cummins.

'No, sadly. This one's close to Hackney Central tube station.'

'That's a very busy area.' The Chief Inspector paused for a moment. 'There must be plenty of security camera's in the vicinity, surely?'

'There are.'

'We need to get them checked out.'

Mason pursed his lips, taking his time before answering. 'That's the second withdrawal in as many days, and both within a two-mile radius of each other. He's definitely local.'

'It would appear so.'

'Someone knows who he is. . . surely?'

Cummins transferred the bundle of case files to his other arm. 'Before I forget, there's been another incident over on the Clapton Park Estate – a young lad was stabbed in the arm last night.'

'What time was this?'

'Around eight o'clock according to the duty desk sergeant.'

The mere mention of another knife attack churned Mason's stomach. It was Sod's Law, something else kicking off at the most inconvenient time. The moment the police had withdrawn from the estate, the gangs had moved back into it again.

'We need more eyes on the estate, Boss.'

'While I admire your enthusiasm, it's me who is answerable. Try not to rush into it. Let's send a couple of PCSOs down there and see what this is all about. It could be part of this recent spate of turf wars that's kicked off, and not an isolated incident.'

'Will do.'

Cummins nodded and started to head off, then swivelled on his heels. 'There is one other thing.'

'Boss?'

'We have a new lad starting on Monday, his name is David Carlisle.'

'What do we know about him?'

'He's an up and coming bright spark according to Superintendent Smyth and has a second-class honours degree in behavioural psychology.'

'Behavioural psychology? Impressive.'

'Open University, I believe. He's ambitious by all accounts and has recently been selected to the Metropolitan's Murder Investigation Team as a criminal psychologist. He's no mug, so he could be very useful to us.'

Mason cocked his head to one side. 'What the hell is he doing here?'

'The people upstairs are keen he gets some hands-on experience.'

'Well. there's plenty of that, for sure.'

'Good. I knew you'd warm to the idea.' Cummins smiled. 'You may wish to take him under your wing for a couple of weeks – familiarise him with the Watkins case. Who knows, his criminal profiling skills may prove to be useful.'

Mason shrugged. 'I could do with an extra pair of hands, that is for sure.'

'Perfect. I'll fill you in with the details later.'

Mason stepped into his office feeling upbeat. He'd been having a rough time lately and was fast running out of ideas. The thought of another pair of willing hands to share his workload pleased him immensely. Things were on the up, and maybe he could spend a little more time at home.

He checked his day diary.

'Anything to report on last night's stabbing, Norwell?' Mason asked.

DC Summers lifted his head above the computer screen and frowned. 'The lad in question is called Paul Siddons, Sarge.'

'That's the first I've heard of it. Why wasn't I informed?'

'It's only just come via the front desk.'

Mason shot Summers a concerned glance. 'Has anyone spoken to him yet?'

'Not from the murder team they haven't. That said, according to the duty officer he was interviewed in hospital prior to being discharged.'

'Do we know what happened exactly?'

'He was attacked by a group of youths over on the Clapton Park Estate.'

'A member of a rival gang, was he?'

'I wouldn't have thought so,' Summers replied, shaking his head. 'Siddons works as a social volunteer. He runs errands for old people and occasionally helps out in the community kitchens. He was stepping out of the tower block lift when the attack took place and walked right into them by all accounts. When he tried to run away, that's when he was stabbed in the arm with a flick-knife.'

Mason felt his eyes narrow.

'A flick-knife! That sounds very much like the bastard who had a go at me.'

'Could be,' Summers acknowledged. 'I know that Stratford are running a stop and search operation called Santa Claus, so it might be worth giving them a call.'

'People who carry flick-knifes don't sit well in my books, Norwell. We need to chase this up, and quick.'

'Uniforms are already on it, Sarge.'

'Good man.'

Mason took down the details and moved towards the long bank of filing cabinets running along the back wall of the office. The way things were going, if they didn't act soon, they could be faced with an even bigger problem. This latest attack had an all too familiar ring about it, and he was determined to get to the bottom of it.

He opened one of the central filing cabinets and flicked through the case folder tabs. Mason's instincts as a working detective over the years had slowly developed with time; he'd acquired a sixth sense for sniffing out rotten apples, and never forgot a face. As he thumbed through dozens of case files, he found the one he was looking for.

Operation Santa Claus.

'Bingo.'

'Found something of interest, Sarge?' asked Summers.

'The young lad who threatened me over on the Clapton Park Estate, his name is Tony Abbott.'

'Never heard of him. I wonder if it's the same guy who set about Paul Siddons?'

'It wouldn't surprise me.'

'I'll get uniforms to pick him up, Sarge. Let's bring him in for questioning.' Summers gave Mason a look of concern. 'We can't have a loose cannon running around. . . he needs to be dealt with good and proper.'

Mason thought about it, and quickly decided against it. Quite often, it wasn't so much what a person did that was revealing, it was the pattern in which they did things that jumped out at you. He smiled at how opposed to rushing into things he was nowadays. Until he had enough evidence to lay more serious charges against Tony Abbott, that is. His plan, inasmuch as he had one, was to catch the Southside Gang leader at his own game. Red-handed if possible.

Still smarting over his close encounter in the tower block lift, Mason let his mind drift. Abbott clearly had an attitude problem, an irresponsible moron with little or no respect for the law. Mason hated parasites at the best of times. Bottom feeders who thrived on attacking the weak and vulnerable and didn't give a toss how many people's lives they ruined along the way. The moment he clapped eyes on Tony Abbott, he knew he would go into one of his red mist rages – God forbid he caught up with him in a dark alley one night.

'Hold fire on Abbott,' Mason insisted. 'I have other plans for him.'

'Like what?' Summers said, looking curious.

'Meet me down in the carpark in five minutes.'

'Where are we going now, Sarge?'

'Hackney Central tube station to check on a cash machine.'

'And after that?'

'My favourite stamping ground.'

'Not the Clapton Hart pub?' The Constable groaned. 'The beer is as weak as piss!'

Mason lifted his eyes to the heavens. Summers was right, it was a crap pint and they'd run out of cheese and onion crisps as he remembered. The one thing it did have going in its favour, though, was that local gossip ran rife in the place.

CHAPTER
TWELVE

Including Jack Mason, there were seven hand-picked officers assembled close to the Lee Navigation. It was a bitterly cold night. Low clouds, little light, with plenty of ground cover. Now fifty meters from their target, Mason surveyed his surroundings as he adjusted his eyes to the dark. A ton of questions needed answering, but that would come later, once Tony Abbott was in custody.

As it had done so many times in the past, intelligence gathering had finally paid dividends. Not for the first time the Anchor and Hope had been of great interest to the police, and a night raid was inevitable. It was Abbott's favourite drinking hole, and Mason hoped to catch the Southside Gang leader red-handed. Concerned about the sudden increase in knife crime on the estate, Mason was looking for answers. Was Tony Abbott involved? Did he stab Paul Siddons? The real problem was that you could hardly go knocking on a suspect's door as they knew you were coming. It was a game of kidology, deliberately lulling a suspect into a false sense of security by pretending to turn a blind eye.

Tucked back in one of the many quiet side streets, a steady stream of police officers now moved into position.

Dressed in their familiar black riot gear and carrying 14-inch batons, they looked a formidable force. Every murder investigation was part of a puzzle, fitting the pieces together was the problem. No two operations were ever the same, and all it took was one bad move. Not on Mason's watch, though. This raid had been fine-tuned, right down to the very last detail. At least they had strength in numbers, always a major plus in these operations.

Laughter reached Mason through the pub's taproom door, coming from the bar. There were twenty of them in total. Late teens mainly, and some a little older. Not surprisingly they chose the Anchor and Hope, given its reputation as a breeding ground for undesirable troublemakers who loved to strut their stuff.

Through a gap in the door, Mason spotted Abbott. He was standing at the bar, pint in hand, and holding court. Dressed in a black hoodie, jeans, and white trainers loosely tied, the gang leader's posture oozed confidence. Mason smiled to himself. He would take him by surprise, put an end to his shenanigans and bring some order back to the streets of Clapton. Not that Abbott would put up much of a fight. The odds were heavily stacked against him, and vermin like Abbott would make a run for it at the first real sniff of trouble.

Mason chose his moment carefully knowing all the exit doors were covered.

'Go, go, go,' he shouted.

As dozens of police officers poured in through the tiniest of gaps in the main entrance door, spontaneous fighting broke out. Fists, arms, legs, anything that could be thrown into the mix was being thrown into it.

Mason heard glass breaking and caught a flash of silver light. He ducked, instinctively, the moment he saw an arm being raised. What followed was a perfectly timed boot to the crotch and the feeling of soft sinking satisfaction. As the youth dropped to his knees, the sergeant stepped over him to get to Abbott.

Mason didn't do things in half measures, it wasn't in his nature. Brought up on a tough council estate, he'd learnt the hard way – leading from the front. Even so, these thugs were made of sterner stuff and surprisingly refusing to yield ground.

Just me and you now, Mason thought.

The sergeant felt the blow, then tasted the blood.

Abbott was goading him, his hand moving ominously towards his knife pocket. But there was nowhere else to go, and he immediately threw himself back into the fray. So many unanswered questions, so many things that didn't add up. Before Abbott had time to react, Mason reached over and grabbed hold of his assailant's collar. It ripped, came away in his hand, and the realisation suddenly sunk in.

'Nab him!' he yelled.

Horrified, Abbott ran towards the taproom door. It wasn't a good move. As a team of angry officers gave chase, the gang leader's downfall seemed inevitable. One officer, a surly bugger by the name of Kevin Hammer, seemed eager to get to him first.

'Over here!' the officer shouted.

Then Mason saw Abbott, scrambling up and over a stack of empty beer crates piled up against a brick wall. He was heading for the yard gate and trying to evade capture.

'Stop him!' Mason yelled. 'He's getting away!'

The moment Abbott cleared the other side, he grabbed hold of the nearest stack of beer crates and began to pull them over.

Everyone froze.

'*Shit!*' someone yelped.

What followed was an almighty crash, as dozens of officers scattered in all directions. The next thing they saw, looking around, was Abbott heading towards the Lee Navigation.

'Don't just stand there,' Mason screamed. 'Get after him!'

Within seconds of picking themselves up, another stack of beer crates came toppling over. Chaos reigned as officers frantically stumbled around in the dark. But Abbott was now in full flight, heading for one of the lock gates and desperately trying to evade capture.

'There!' Someone screamed. 'He's running along the towpath.'

CHAPTER
THIRTEEN

Mason didn't carry a torch, a decision he now regretted. He led half a dozen uniformed officers, sprinting along the towpath running parallel with the river, and making good progress. It was ink-dark, the only light came from the occupied narrowboats moored alongside the canal, the distant streetlights of Upper Clapton, and the barest reflection of the moon on the water.

Cursing his luck, there was something too final in the direction that Abbot was heading. To his left was a row of terraced cottages, to his right the canal known as the Lee Navigation. Mason could see a long string of narrowboats moored up, some occupied, others dark and empty. Now thinking about the charges, he would throw at his suspect, he tried to focus his mind. He would take Abbott by force, overpower him, and bring an end to his violent reign of terror.

Glancing round, Mason could see a posse of police officers trailing in his wake. He recognised that Abbott was ten years younger than many of them, but they were weighed down by police equipment and struggling to keep up.

Mason increased his pace.

He thought for an instant about Brenda. Of their unborn child. About being a father. He could see the gap was closing between them and swore he could hear Abbott wheezing. Was he carrying a flick-knife? Had he thrown it away? He hoped not as it was the one piece of evidence he was looking for.

His mind all over the place, they turned sharply, away from the canal, and into Springfield Park. Bounded by trees on either side, tracks criss-crossed in all directions. It wasn't a good place to give chase. It had an ominous feel, intimidating, as if Abbott could turn on him at any moment.

Still in his sights, somewhere in the night he heard the wail of a police car siren. Faint at first, but distinctly getting louder. To his left, the heavily built up Clapton Common estate, to his right the Lee Navigation. As the ground in front of him opened up, he could see dozens of flashlights heading towards them. They were moving at speed in a long sweeping arc, he guessed it was backup.

'You're completely surrounded,' Mason yelled at the top of his voice.

He'd stopped running now – only breathless panting over his shoulder could be heard. He turned, sharply, and saw PC Sheila White lumbering towards him. She carried a flashlamp in her hand, which kept bobbing up and down as she ran.

'He's hiding around the other side, Sarge,' White called out.

'I see him,' another yelled out.

It didn't take long.

Picked out in White's flashlight beam, Abbott was cowering in thick undergrowth. Now surrounded on all sides by dozens of angry police officers, the Southside Gang leader looked decidedly sorry for himself.

It was over – well, not quite.

Mason approached with caution. 'Tony Abbot, I'm arresting you on suspicion of murder. You do not have to say anything, but it may harm your defence if you do not mention when questioned something you later rely on in court. Anything you do say may be given in evidence.'

'Don't spout that bullshit at me, you know I'm innocent!'

'Try telling that to a jury,' Mason groaned.

At that point, Mason didn't care what Abbott had to say. Furious, he slid a pair of handcuffs around the gang leader's scrawny wrist and continued with his search. Spinning Abbott round, he felt for the flick-knife. It was hidden in the suspect's left trouser pocket.

'Is this the same knife you threatened me with?'

Abbott looked at him stony-faced. 'It's for peeling apples.'

'Big fucking apples,' Mason replied, dropping it into a plastic forensic bag. 'Let's hope this doesn't have traces of Paul Siddons' blood on it.'

'Never heard of him.'

'He's the guy you stabbed over on the Clapton Park estate – remember?'

'Don't crap me.'

'We'll soon see about that.'

The moment they frogmarched Abbott away to a waiting police van, Mason breathed a sigh of relief. It was over, and he was finally back in control again. But would his suspect talk? Would he name the killer? That was the million-dollar question on everyone's lips.

Back inside the Anchor and Hope, the pub resembled a bomb site. Glass everywhere, overturned tables and chairs, it had been one hell of a fight. More than pleased with the way his team had handled themselves, Mason tried to relax. With most of the Southside Gang now rounded up, there seemed little point in going after the stragglers. That would come later, once they had a list of those involved.

The taproom door opened and a head appeared.

'Another good day at the office, Sarge?' Constable Summers grinned.

'You could say that,' Mason nodded.

Summers looked at his watch. 'There's not a lot more we can do here, Sarge.'

'No, I suppose not.'

'Why don't you leave it with us to clear up?' DC Crawford said, looking decidedly pleased with himself. 'There's nothing that we can't handle.'

His mind all over the place, Mason pocketed his notebook. There were statements to be gathered, reports to write, but that could be done in the morning. Above all else, he was itching to get home and find out how Brenda's day had gone.

Mason glanced at Crawford. 'What about the rest of the Southside Gang?'

'It'll take all night to book them in. Besides, they ain't going anywhere fast.'

'No, I suppose not.'

'Well, then?'

Mason hesitated. 'I'll leave you two to get on with it, then?'

Chambers smiled and gave him a thumbs up. 'See you in the morning, Sarge.'

Just before he left, Mason handed Summers Tony Abbott's flick-knife. Fortunately, the Southside Gang leader hadn't tossed it into the river like he thought he might have. With any luck they now had enough incriminating evidence to put Abbott behind bars for a very long time. Crimes solved was a good thing; unsolved crimes a bad thing. It was possible that Abbott wasn't involved in Harold Watkins' murder at all, but he was definitely involved in serious knife crime.

Mason smiled as he closed the bar door behind him and made for the unmarked police car. If he put his foot down, he could be home in twenty-five minutes. He took out his phone, punched in the number, and waited for the dialling tone to kick in.

'It's me darling, I'm on my way home.'

'Not much happening tonight?' Brenda replied.

'No. It's all been relatively quiet if I'm––'

'Good. I'll order a takeaway.'

His phone went dead.

CHAPTER
FOURTEEN

Jack Mason leaned forward and rested his arms on the interview table. Charged with three counts of carrying a bladed article in a public place, including stabbing Paul Siddons with intent to cause serious injury, Tony Abbott's demeanour looked strained. The Southside Gang leader was now in serious trouble and facing a potential long prison sentence. And, needless to say, the wall of silence that had held firm on the Clapton Park Estate had finally broken down. Residents were talking again and a bigger picture had emerged.

The moment DCI Cummins entered Interview Room One (IR-1), the suspect's body stiffened. Now facing another gruelling round of questions, the atmosphere was tense. Although Abbott's fingerprints had never been found in Harold Watkins flat, it didn't mean he was innocent. They had a potential killer in custody, and they were eager to get to the truth.

'Your mother rang,' the Chief Inspector said. 'She was asking after you.'

'She'd be the last person to talk to you,' said Abbott. 'She hates the filth.'

Cummins brow furrowed. 'Charged with intent to cause serious injury means you could be facing a very long time behind bars. It's not looking good, especially now that new evidence has come to light regarding the attack on Paul Siddons.'

'Who the fuck is Siddons?'

'The young man you stabbed over on the Clapton Park Estate. Remember?'

'Oh yeah! Try pulling the other fucking leg.'

IR-1 fell silent, the atmosphere strained.

'For the purposes of the tape, I'm showing Mr Abbot exhibit B356.'

Cummins slid a monochrome photograph in front of Abbot. 'At 8:30 pm on the evening of the twenty-seventh, you were seen stepping out of a lift on the Clapton Park Estate when you attacked Paul Siddons with a bladed weapon. This knife,' Cummins said, tapping the photograph with his finger.

'No comment.'

'This is your knife, is it not?'

'No comment,' Abbot replied angrily.

'We know you were in the vicinity of the Clapton Park Estate at the time that Paul Siddons was stabbed, and we have eyewitness accounts to back that up.'

'So, what! I live there.'

Cummins thought a moment. 'Tell me about this Southside Gang you're involved in. Is it true you are their leader?'

'No comment!'

'Here's the thing,' said Cummins, visibly annoyed. 'We also have several witness accounts which state that you were involved in the recent spate of stabbings on the estate.'

'That's bullshit!'

'The problem is, a man who carries a flick-knife around in his pocket all day and isn't scared to use it, says an awful lot about that person's character. We're not daft. You may think we are, but we're not.'

The young man shrugged, refusing to meet either officer's eyes.

Cummins eased back in his seat and looked hard at Abbott. 'You're going to have to start cooperating with us, because you're not making a very good job of it. The fact is, we now have compelling evidence that puts you in the vicinity of Harold Watkins' flat around the time the old man was attacked.'

'No comment.'

'Being a gang leader is all about building a reputation and showing the other gang members just how tough you are. Isn't that what this is all about?'

Abbott hunched his shoulders in an aggressive pose. 'If you're trying to scare me, it ain't working.'

'No, I didn't think it would. I just thought I'd mention it, that's all.'

'Fuck you.'

Cummins smiled, his words still resonating around the room. There was a cold calculating intensity in the chief inspector's voice. He was good, extremely good, and his delivery impeccable, Mason thought.

'Let's talk about this murder charge you are up against.'

Abbott squirmed in his seat. He was shaking, and desperately trying to hide the fact. 'Why bother? You know I didn't do it.'

'Do what?'

'Beat the old geezer up.'

'Really?' Cummins smiled. 'Try telling a jury that when my sergeant informs them you tried to stab him to death whilst he was on duty.'

'Nice try,' Abbott squirmed.

Mason felt a cold shudder wash over him. The chief inspector's masterly approach had certainly got under Abbott's skin, and it was showing. What he did have in abundance, though, was egotism.

'Why don't you tell me what really took place in Harold Watkins' flat that day?'

Abbott shrugged. 'Cos.'

'Cos, what?'

'Cos I've told you all I know.'

'What about my sergeant here. Are you saying he's lying?'

'It was self-defence – everyone saw him punch me first.'

'That's not how I see it,' said Mason, drumming the tabletop with his fingers.

'Oh yeah? What about the other ten dudes who were there? Are you saying they're stupid?'

'There were six of you, actually.'

'Don't bullshit me––'

Cummins cut across them. 'Do you think my sergeant is lying?'

'I know he's fucking lying, cos that's what you bastards are taught to do.'

'Try telling that to a jury when I show them the CCTV footage of you pointing a knife at his throat.'

Abbott drew back in his seat. 'It's bollocks.'

Cummins shook his head and sighed. 'I never joke about anything involving the law, Tony. Three innocent people. All attacked in the same building and all by the same group of youths.'

'What are you trying to say?'

'The evidence speaks for itself. First Harold Watkins, then a police officer on duty, and now Paul Siddons.'

Abbott sank into his seat looking decidedly deflated.

'I need names,' said Cummins forcefully. 'That's how the system operates around here. You help me, and I'll see what I can do for you.'

'Don't shit me, motherfucker. I've told you all I know.'

'Names, Tony. I need names.'

Cummins seemed to concentrate on the logic. He was sharp, direct, and cut through the suspect's defences with ease. He knew how to handle people caught up in awkward situations, and it was enough to put the fear of God into many a grown man.

The chief inspector scooted his chair. 'Now here's my problem. You and your so-called cronies were seen in the vicinity around the time the old man's flat was broken into. It's what's known as indirect evidence. . . evidence that does not directly prove a fact in dispute but allows a jury to draw reasonable inference that puts you close to the crime scene. Your biggest concern right now is that we have enough evidence to put you inside the old man's property at the time of the attack.'

'Impossible. You're full of shit.'

'Well,' said Cummins leaning back in his chair and linking his hands behind his head with a calculating coldness. 'Like I say, we're not daft. That's why we're currently searching your mother's property.'

Abbott shook his head in disbelief. 'Don't fuck with me.'

'It's what we do best, Tony. Whilst you're banged up here in a cosy police cell with a roof over your head and three-square meals a day, we can't just sit around waiting for you to come to your senses.'

Abbott spoke aggressively. 'This is bad shit. . . tell me you're joking.'

'It's not a game. Far from it. It's a fact.'

'Screw you. You're bluffing.'

Having spoken very little throughout, Abbott's solicitor leaned over and said. 'You have no evidence to link my client to any crime – can't prove he was inside the victim's flat, nor that he assaulted Paul Siddons. In fact, the only thing you seem to have, is that he was in possession of a knife...'

Mason shot Abbott a withering glance. 'The trouble is yours is the only name in the frame. So, unless you can come up with a better explanation as to who killed Harold Watkins, it's you who will take the rap.'

As guilty as hell, Abbott was fighting it every inch of the way.

'You heard my brief,' Abbott smiled. 'You ain't got nothing on me.'

Cummins pushed his chair back and stood to his feet. Hands in pockets, head hunched slightly forward, he glowered at Abbott. 'I can't see any point in us continuing. So, unless you have something of interest to tell us, I'm terminating the interview.'

Abbott glared at Cummins, and for a moment Mason thought he was going to kick off. He didn't. Instead he leaned back in his chair, linked his hands behind his head and started to laugh. 'You're bullshitting me––'

'It's not a game, Tony,' Mason interrupted.

Abbott struggled to get his words out. 'Don't crap me. You know it wasn't me.'

Mason leaned in closer. 'Okay. The day I met you in the service lift, where had you been?'

Abbott paused so long before answering that Mason thought he'd not understood the question. 'We was up on the roof – we hang out there.'

Abbott's voice sounded monotone, disconnected, as if forcing his words.

'And what were you doing there?'

Abbott laughed out brashly. 'We was looking for a rumble.'

'A fight?'

'Yeah. . . we can see everything that's happening up there.'

'Eyes in the sky, eh.' Cummins smiled. 'Tell me, what *did* you see that day?'

'Not a lot.'

'What do you mean. . . not a lot?'

'We saw dozens of cherries and berries arriving and decided to get our arses out of it.' Abbott paused in thought. 'That's when we met your sergeant here.'

Cummins scowled. 'So, why threaten him with a knife?'

'He threw me a punch, remember.'

Mason felt a cold shudder running down his spine. Wrong place, right time, he suspected. At least Abbott was talking, which was more than they'd bargained for. Perhaps they'd been a little too harsh on him. If he was telling the truth, what then? They would need a fresh approach. Something more concrete. Who else was in the vicinity around the time the old man's flat was broken into?

Cummins leaned forward in his seat.

'Let's talk about this rooftop viewing point. How many of you were up there?'

'Don't remember.'

Abbott's answer was vague, and Cummins had picked up on it. 'Someone broke into the old man's flat, and we suspect it was you.'

'Jesus. You ain't been listening to me.'

'Why can't it be you? You seem to know an awful lot about what's going on in the estate.'

'I ain't the fucking Thames House.'

'And yet you conveniently missed my sergeant's arrival on the scene.'

Mason bit his lip, as he wrote something down.

'I tell you what,' said Abbott, looking extremely annoyed. 'If I had beaten the shit out of the old geezer like you said I did then everyone on the estate would have known about it.'

'What makes you say that?'

Abbott spoke to his solicitor again, who turned to face them. 'It's known as street credibility, Chief Inspector.'

'Ah, yes. Street cred! I'd almost forgotten about that.'

'It's how others judge you.'

'Yes, I know. But try telling that to dozens of mothers who have lost their sons caught up in knife crime over the years.'

Cummins eyed Abbott up, leaned over and switched the interview recording tape off.

'If you claim to be the eyes and ears of the estate, then surely you must have a few names in mind?'

'It ain't that simple, and you know it.'

'So, we're back to this street credibility thing again?'

'Yeah, right first time for once.'

CHAPTER
FIFTEEN

Mason peered over the rooftop balcony at Ambergate Court and felt a cold blast of air in his face. Twenty storeys up, with commanding views overlooking the whole of Clapton Park Estate, there was little wonder Tony Abbott had chosen this particular vantage point. But the city had changed so much, even in Mason's brief lifetime. He could remember, as a child, when streets like these were safe to play in. Not anymore. Estates had been carved up into various, bitter, postcode rivalries, and child criminal exploitation was the new growing buzzword. It wasn't good, and the younger gang members, between the ages of twelve and sixteen, were becoming increasingly active in street crime.

He watched as another forensic van joined the cluster of parked police cars. There was still plenty of activity on the estate even though things had quietened down a tad.

'Thinking of throwing yourself off?' said David Carlisle, as he strode to join him.

Mason smiled. 'Pushing someone over, more like.'

'Did Bob Cummins say anything to you about me sitting in on the next Abbott interview?'

'Yes, he did.'

'What are your thoughts?'

'Anything's worth a try.' Mason replied.

Having gone back over the Abbott interview transcripts, Carlisle's criminal profiling skills offered another dimension to their investigations. Cummins was keen on the idea, and Mason was happy to string along if it meant progress.

'What's your take on it?' asked Carlisle.

'We need to establish what the North Boys' leader is up to,' Mason said, turning to face the profiler. 'There's a rabbit off somewhere, and I can't put my finger on it.'

'What do we know about him?'

'Brian Fagan, aka Zelly, previously lived with an aunt in Peckham. He excelled at school and was doing really well for himself by all accounts. Three years ago, he suddenly dropped off the radar and ended up here on the estate. He's not very well liked apparently and has earned a fearful reputation amongst local residents.'

'So, why Clapton Park of all places. What's the attraction?'

'He got in with the wrong crowd of people apparently – running errands for a bigtime crook who'd taken a shine to him. One thing for sure, he's one step ahead of the game and knows how to play the system.'

Carlisle dug his hands in his pockets and shrugged. 'I got the impression the Southside Gang leader thinks Zelly's a bit of an idiot.'

Mason grinned. 'Zelly's not daft, he just comes across that way at times.'

'Interesting,' Carlisle said, thoughtfully.

'I wouldn't trust him as far as I could throw him.'

'Stupid people do tend to overestimate their competence, while smart people often sell themselves short.'

'Zelly's smart all right, he's not the idiot that some people make him out to be.'

'Could someone be pulling Zelly's strings?' Carlisle quizzed.

'It's possible. But who, is the question?'

'The man obviously has ambitions, hence his fearless reputation.'

Mason shook his head in despair. 'Zelly controls a group of young thugs known as the North Boys. Hooligans mainly, young offenders who don't give a damn about the local community. They're a pain in the arse, but the real issue is the two warring gangs are constantly at each other's throats. Drugs mainly, and disputes over territory rights.'

'Turf wars,' said Carlisle, shaking his head. 'So, Zelly runs the north side of the estate and Abbott the south side.'

'In a nutshell, yes.'

'So, why does Abbott despise Zelly? Is he the more dominant figure?'

'The hatred between them runs deep,' Mason explained. 'It's a power struggle, they both want control of each other's territory. Maybe there's a darker side to all of this, one that has yet to surface.'

Carlisle acknowledged with a shake of the head. 'What's Tony Abbott's background? What do we know about him?'

'The man has a serious hatred towards authority in any shape or form. In and out of prison from the age of ten, his main offences include drugs, house breaking, GBH, and car theft or twocking, as it is better known. He's not the friendliest person to deal with and has recently developed a propensity towards serious knife crime.'

'An ideal candidate for murder, it would seem.'

'I'm not convinced about that, but he does have a violent streak in him. I can certainly vouch for that. A few weeks back, the bastard tried to have a go at me and came pretty close to succeeding might I add.' Mason gathered his thoughts. 'Mind, I don't think he was involved in the Watkins murder, it's not his style. Abbott's more interested in maintaining his street image. It's a reputation thing, and knife crime fits his cause perfectly.'

'What about firearms, is he known to have used them?'

'Not that I'm aware of.'

'Fascinating,' said Carlisle. 'Two warring gang leaders doesn't bode well for good harmony on the estate.'

Mason blew through his teeth. 'Tell me about it.'

'How does Abbott come across during interviews?'

'He's difficult to weigh up if I'm honest, as he constantly blows hot and cold.' Mason shrugged. 'He's better off behind bars in my opinion, he's a troublemaker.'

'Sounds like we have a real problem on our hands.'

Mason had never been keen on the principle of good guy-bad guy interviews. He'd used them before with little effect. Abbott was a slippery customer who would turn on a sixpence if he thought he could get away with it. Having threatened Abbott with a lengthy prison sentence if he refused to talk, Mason was hoping it would play on the gang leader's mind. Sometimes psychology worked, other times not. It was a fine balancing act, and you never knew which way the wind would blow. The problem was, unlike a thief who could pay his – or her – victim's compensation, murder could never be undone. It was final, and always left a nasty taste in the mouth.

'We need to gain Abbott's trust,' said Carlisle thoughtfully.

'What if he turns inwards on you? What then?'

'I've studied the transcripts, and he already has.'

'How did you work that one out?'

'Entering an interview room assuming guilt means you're only listening to certain parts of the evidence. It's selective listening in my view and tends to ignore the things that don't fit with your script.'

Mason shook his head feebly. 'You've obviously done your homework, but I don't share your views unfortunately. What I can tell you is, we've gone over Abbott's bedroom with a fine-tooth comb and nothing of interest has shown up.' Mason swung sharply to face Carlisle. 'If Abbott isn't responsible for Harold Watkins' murder, he may know someone who is.'

'Threatening him will get you nowhere, you've already established that. The problem is, the harder you try the more he will resist you.'

Mason ran his fingers through his short-cropped hair. 'I'm not trying to force the bastard into making a confession, for God's sake. Abbott is holding back on something. I'm convinced of that.'

'Forcing him to talk is never going to work.' Carlisle looked hard at him. 'If he wears his criminal record pinned to his chest like a badge of honour, he'll resist you all the way.'

'So, how do you intend to approach the interview?'

'Thugs like Abbott see themselves as role models – they have deluded opinions about how society sees them. It's all about respect, making them feel important. That's how you get them to open up.'

'What Abbott needs is a good size nine boot up the arse.'

'True, but conflict will only enhance his reputation.'

'Tell me,' said Mason, spinning on his heels. 'How do you propose to break the cycle if Abbott refuses to cooperate?'

'In the wider personality structure, his persona plays an important role in the complexities of motivation. On the surface Abbott portrays himself as the hard man, but beneath the veneer I suspect lies a less confident personality.'

Mason laughed. 'I'm not so sure about that.'

Carlisle cocked his head to one side in thought. 'The question you should be asking yourself is, which side of the fence is Abbott sitting on? Is this a power struggle, or is he trying to protect himself from something?'

'Or someone,' Mason cut in.

'And we know he'd dearly love to take control of Zelly's northside.'

Mason grinned. 'In other words, what influences does the North Boys' leader hold over him?'

'Exactly.'

Mason had never worked with a criminal profiler before and offender profiling was a subject he knew nothing about. Despite the lack of scientific research, profiling was a highly regarded tool in US law enforcement agencies. Carlisle's methodology intrigued him, particularly the concept of linkage analysing. He might not be sure about the science behind it, but Mason didn't give a damn if it meant it uncovered Watkins' killer.

Two hundred feet below, another marked patrol car drove off the forecourt. There were still a lot of police activity in the area, and they were certainly making their presence felt. As they moved towards the service lift together, Mason wished he shared the profiler's enthusiasm. Abbott would be a difficult nut to crack, no doubting that. Even so, if DCI Cummins couldn't get him to open up, could a criminal profiler succeed?

Anything was possible.

The lift stank of disinfectant and vomit. Nothing ever changed, Mason groaned. He pressed the descent button and watched as the green digital display began to count the floor levels down. Strangely enough, Carlisle seemed confidently upbeat about his impending interview with Abbott, even though the two had never met. Mason just hoped Abbott's solicitor would have warned his client against going "no-comment" on them. Murder interviews were strange affairs at the best of times, as you never knew how the suspect would react. Bluffing was key to many a winning hand, and cross-examination felt like a game of poker in many ways. Tomorrow was another day, and he would need to keep an open mind about the outcome.

As Mason and Carlisle drove out of the forecourt and past security, the first spots of rain hit the car's windscreen. It was cold enough for snow, but thankfully a jet stream was blowing warmer air in from the south of France and pushing everything north. Eager to get back to his office, Mason still had a mountain of paperwork to climb. Not that he was looking forward to it. He wasn't.

Although most of the Southside Gang members were facing an uncertain future, he was hoping that one of them might talk. Pressure got to people, made them nervous, and forced them to open up. But having spent most of his life walking these streets, he knew how most low-life operated.

Scumbags, every single one of them!

CHAPTER SIXTEEN

As far as Jack Mason was concerned, the profiler's interview with Tony Abbott hadn't got off to a good start. Highly intelligent, Carlisle had a sharp retentive mind but his delivery was far too measured and seldom kept to the script. Nothing wrong with that, but time was a luxury in this game and you had to use it sparingly. In truth, they were poles apart in their approach to resolving Harold Watkins' murder – but he still had faith in the profiler's ability to win Abbott over at some stage.

Carlisle showed Abbott several stills from the CCTV footage.

'Do you know this man, Mr Abbott?'

The gang leader shrugged, and Mason tried not to scowl. It looked like the profiler was going to have to work harder to get information.

'No comment.'

'When I was your age, I was scared of the bad guys. It never gets any easier, does it. Always worried someone will see through the brave face, eh?' Carlisle smiled warmly as he eased back in his seat. 'It's a confidence thing, something that sticks in your mind and triggers the nightmares.'

Abbott's eyes were all over the place.

'I haven't the foggiest idea what you're banging on about.'

'But I do know fear when I see it,' Carlisle replied.

'I'm not scared of shit.'

'I know.' Carlisle leaned forward, elbows on the table. 'I was looking through a photograph album we found in your bedside cabinet the other day. There was a picture of you and your father in it, and you were walking along a beach looking at sailing ships together. Much happier times, I suspect – a long time ago. Tell me, what kind of man was your father?'

'What's my old man got to do with it?'

Abbott was fighting his demons, unsure of which way to turn. Hands clasped on the table in front of him, he seemed ill at ease, Mason thought.

'I know how it is,' said Carlisle, calmly. 'Without a father figure it's always difficult to seek advice when you need it most. Tell me, why is Zelly such a threat to you?'

Mason thought he caught a faint flicker, a subtle sign that Carlisle was on to something.

'Zelly don't scare me.'

'Of course not. But there is a reason for your nightmares, Tony. I get it. I have them too. I'm terrified that they'll find out I'm faking this, that I'm some sort of phoney.'

Mason couldn't tell if Carlisle's smile was for him or Abbott.

'Bullshit. You don't know anything about me,' the Southside Gang leader glowered.

'Do you think you can handle it?'

'Who said I couldn't?'

'What about the North Boys, do they give you much grief?'

Abbott hesitated before answering. 'I'm not scared of shit.'

'That's the second time you've said that,' Mason cut in.

Carlisle pointed down at the photographs again. 'This man at the cash machine. He's one of Zelly's gang members, isn't he?'

'Never seen him before.'

Mason leaned forward and tapped a finger on the metal tabletop. 'You're still under caution, Abbott. And why are you protecting him? Does Zelly have something on you, or is this a loyalty thing between fellow gang leaders?'

'You ain't listening,' Abbott snarled.

'How could someone get hold of the credit card?' asked Mason. 'Did they steal it from a defenceless old man? Is that how Zelly's gang operate – picking on the vulnerable?'

Abbott shrugged, but said nothing.

'You can't go on fighting it,' Carlisle cut in. 'You're much better than Zelly.'

'You know nothing about what I'm thinking.'

'Oh, but I do. And that worries me.'

'So, you think you can read my mind?'

'I know I can.'

'Bollocks.'

The profiler gestured to the photograph again. He was playing with Abbott's mind, trying to unsettle him and get inside the gang leader's head. It was a clever ruse.

'Something is bothering you and, whatever it is, you need to let it go. If not, it will spark off all kinds of weird and wonderful emotions inside your head.'

Abbott looked at Carlisle hard. 'Oh, yeah? The minute I tell you bastards anything you'll use it against me as evidence.'

Mason waved a finger at Abbott. 'Not this time, Tony. It could work in your favour.'

'It's all talk.'

'Tell me about Zelly,' said Carlisle softly. 'Why do you despise him?'

Abbott's solicitor leaned over and interrupted them. 'At this point I would like to have a few words with my client, if I may.'

'Go ahead,' Mason said, as he switched off the interview tape. 'Take your time, you've got plenty of that on your hands.'

Suddenly the opportunity for plea bargaining became more apparent, as if their suspect was about to open up. It didn't take long, and within minutes of them leaving IR-1, the two detectives were summoned back in again.

'My client wishes to make a statement,' Abbott's solicitor announced.

'Really?'

'Before that happens, I need assurances that some of the charges can be dropped.'

'Which charges are these?' Mason said.

'The one's involving Harold Watkins' murder.'

Mason's mind went blank, as if some geek had hacked into his brain and scrambled everything up. Smiling at them, trying to think of something that would sound positive, he reached for his notes. Something didn't sit right. Abbott's solicitor, who had said very little throughout, had suddenly taken centre stage. Why? What was he up to?

Pen poised, Mason stared hard at Abbott's solicitor. 'It depends on what your client is about to tell us, of course. Off the record, I presume we are talking joint enterprise here?'

Abbott's solicitor nodded. 'I can assure you my client had nothing to do with Harold Watkins' death, but he may have some important information that may be of major interest to you.'

'I'm all ears,' Mason smiled. 'I take it your client was in the vicinity of Harold Watkins' flat at the time the attack took place?'

'No, he wasn't.'

'In which case we'd better hear what he has to say for himself.'

Abbott squirmed in his seat as Mason switched on the interview tape. It was all about trust, and there was very little of that in the room. The tension was mounting, and the sergeant was on tenterhooks.

'Okay. Take your time. Tell us what you know.'

Abbott's solicitor drew in a long intake of air and scooted his seat. 'It's my understanding that Brian Fagan, aka Zelly, has a half-brother called John Martin who lives on a narrowboat, called *Kingfisher*. Travelling the length and breadth of the Lee Navigation, Martin is heavily involved in the trafficking of illegal drugs coming out of London Docks.'

Mason looked at Carlisle then at Abbott. 'Is this true, Tony?'

Abbott shrugged. 'Yeah. Zelly and his half-bruv are in it together.'

'They're dealers?'

'Yeah. That's how most of the big H hits the estate.'

Mason took stock. Unfortunately, John Martin's name didn't flag up any immediate concerns. Of major interest though, was Martin a possible link to Harold Watkins' murder. Was Abbott telling the truth? Or was he trying to pull the wool over their eyes in order to get one over his arch-rival?

'I'm missing something here,' said Mason, fidgeting awkwardly. 'If you had nothing to do with Harold Watkins' murder, then who did?'

'Zelly and his half-bruv Martin.'

'Really? What makes you say that?'

Abbot laughed. 'I knew Zelly was flooding the estate with drugs. Shit was everywhere and nobody was buying. That's when I found out who was supplying him.'

'Okay,' Carlisle said, scratching his head. 'So how do you know they were involved in a murder?'

'We was out steaming the estate one night, me and the boys, when we bumped into one of Zelly's runners.'

'What happened exactly?'

Abbott glared at Mason, then inclined his head towards Carlisle. 'He was bang out of order. Wrong place, right time.'

'What do you mean by that?' asked Mason.

'The little shit wasn't carrying.'

Mason smiled at Abbott's descriptive narration. 'You mean Zelly's pusher had no drugs on him?'

'Yeah. He was clean.'

Abbott ran the flat of his hand over his head. He was beginning to open up, and Mason was keen for him to continue. 'Tell me about him. What happened next?'

'When I asked what he was doing on our turf, he told me he was about to make a plastic drop.'

'Do you mean a credit card withdrawal?'

'Yeah, man.'

'Whose credit card?' asked Mason.

'He claimed it was Zelly's.'

'And was it?'

'Nah. Zelly's dumb. He can't handle plastic. We knew then it was nicked.'

'Clever,' Carlisle said. 'So, whose card was it?'

There was another long pause between them, a coming together of minds.

'Me thinks it was the old geezer who was iced.'

'What? Harold Watkins?'

'Yeah! Summat like that.'

Carlisle slid the photographs across the table towards Abbott. 'Was this the man who was making the withdrawal?'

'Could be,' Abbott shrugged. 'It's difficult innit.'

'How's that?'

'He's wearing a hoodie.'

'What else can you tell me?' Mason asked.

'That's all I know.'

Abbott clearly had attitude, but his story made sense. It was credible, right down to the credit card withdrawal. Mason leaned over, switched off the interview tape, and turned to Abbott's solicitor. 'Let's hope your client's story rings true.'

'It's true all right. I can assure you of that.'

Mason smiled. 'Good. We understand each other perfectly then.'

'Indeed, we do,' Abbott's solicitor nodded.

CHAPTER
SEVENTEEN

Mason squinted in the morning light. A cold mist hung over the canal, blurring the long string of narrowboats. He wasn't used to being up this early and he hadn't slept enough either. Hands in pockets, head bend slightly forward, he sucked in the air and stared south to the single lock known as Alfie's Lock. He could see a team of police officers making steady progress along a narrow towpath, towards the William Girling Reservoir. Following in their wake, a small "snatch and grab" party was struggling to keep up with them. Two officers carried heavy battering rams slung low across their chests, one a coil of rope, and three lugged circular AM2 riot shields.

Then through the swirling dawn haze, Mason spotted *Kingfisher*. Tied to securing rings and facing north, she was clearly in need of some restoration. What nobody knew, not even him, was if John Martin was onboard. He'd heard rumours he was, and he'd been seen in the vicinity the previous evening, but that didn't mean a thing. Not now it didn't. Mason had made the decision and there was no turning back.

Further north, beyond a bend in the river, another police unit sat hugging the treeline, awaiting the order to move in if required.

'How's it looking?'

Mason turned as DCI Cummins strode to join him.

'Any minute now, Boss.'

'She looks deserted.'

'There's been a hard frost,' Mason replied, reassuringly, 'and Martin may have battened down the hatches to stay warm.'

'Let's hope you're right.'

There was so much resting on this operation, so much at stake.

Mason held the lapels of his overcoat over his throat as he gazed at *Kingfisher*. Sat low in the waterline, there were only two routes their suspect could take – the front and aft galley doors. Both would be rammed simultaneously. And, if Martin did carry a gun, armed officers would deal with it. But he wasn't a shooter according to intelligence, just a nasty felon who prayed on the vulnerable and weak.

Of all the people he was itching to get his hands on, it was John Martin. The man was a social parasite who didn't give a damn how many people's lives he destroyed. Drug trafficking was a lucrative business, and that's all that mattered to him. Not all would be plain sailing, though. There were still a few operational hurdles to overcome. But Mason was confident that most of the groundwork had been done. It was down to Lady Luck.

The canal was silent. Only the sound of creaking mooring ropes.

'*All units standby--*' the call came over the airwaves.

Mason gave the signal.

'*Go, go,*' the lead officer shouted.

The narrowboat doors burst inwards with a bang, and both teams rushed forward with a sense of urgency.

Mason could hear glass breaking, followed by shouting, but still could not see a thing. As the snatch team swept through the narrowboat's living quarters, the racket they made was deafening. Unwelcome noise confused people, disoriented their sense of judgement and caused them to unwittingly panic.

A group of officers peered out from the narrowboat's bow door. One of them shook his head. Martin was nowhere to be seen.

Shit, shit, shit, Mason cursed.

The detective sergeant clambered onboard, closely followed by Cummins. The stench that hit them – like rotten cabbages – was unbearable. Whoever lived here had no regard for hygiene, let alone any sense of order. The place was a tip. Clothes strewn everywhere, a sink piled high with dirty dishes, and every inch of the floor knee-deep in empty food containers.

'Touch nothing,' Cummins instructed.

'No chance of that happening. The place isn't fit for pigs.'

'Which means he may not be far away.'

'Christ! Who'd want to live in this dump?'

The chief inspector's eyes narrowed. 'You need to get forensics down here, and quick.'

Still retching from the unbearable stench, Mason tried the light switch. It didn't work. He slid the curtains back and allowed light to flood in through a porthole. After a few seconds, a voice crackled over the radio waves.

Mason identified himself and gave out instructions.

'What's happening?' asked Cummins.

'It's Jim Brown the police photographer, Boss. He's on his way.'

'Good. The quicker the better.'

It had all sounded so simple on paper, but nothing was ever straightforward during these operations. Get it wrong, and you were nobody's friend, least of all the Chief Inspector's. This was Mason's first real opportunity to impress, a chance to make a real difference. He'd made mistakes but was willing to take ownership and that's all that mattered to him. It was all part of the learning curve, and he was learning fast.

Mason pointed to a short wooden shaft propped against the galley wall.

'What do you think this is, Boss?'

'It's a tiller handle used to steer the narrowboat.'

'Better not touch it. Who knows, it could be a potential murder weapon.'

Cummins nodded. 'It needs to be fast-tracked through the system.'

'I'll get forensics involved.'

'Good man.'

Mason caught movement through the porthole window.

'It seems someone is watching us.'

'Yes. I spotted him earlier,' Cummins replied, unconcerned.

The chief inspector moved back from the window, the sound of his footsteps echoing like the sound of a drum. This was the first time that Mason had worked in the field with Bob Cummins, and he was impressed. Incredibly relaxed, nothing escaped his attention.

'What the hell's he up to?'

'The minute we challenge him, he'll be gone.'

'Should we get the dog teams involved?'

Cummins shook his head as he climbed the narrowboat steps. 'No. He could be a curious onlooker, who knows. Once forensics has completed a sweep of the area, we can post a couple of sentries down here.'

'I doubt Martin will return.'

'If he has any sense he won't. Then again, who knows what lies hidden inside *Kingfisher*.'

Stepping on to dry land, Mason's nerves were on edge. Twenty minutes earlier this had been such a peaceful location; not anymore. It was strange how some operations could suddenly escalate beyond imagination. One minute everything was under control, the next it was up in the air.

'I'll leave you to get on with it,' Cummins said, heading off along the towpath towards the lock keeper's house. 'Let me know how you get on.'

'Will do, Boss.'

As far as the eye could see, police officers were scouring the riverbanks in search of clues. Soon every dwelling and outbuilding along the Lee Navigation would be taken apart in the hunt for John Martin. Nowhere would be safe anymore, no matter where he ran.

CHAPTER

EIGHTEEN

Now gathered in Meeting Room One, there was still no feedback as to John Martin's whereabouts. It was half-past six in the evening, and most of the team had spent the best part of the day chasing shadows. News travelled fast and all the national media channels were running the Lee Navigation incident. It didn't take long, and once reporters got their teeth into a story word soon got around.

Mason took out his notebook and pen as Cummins addressed the assembled team.

'Okay,' the Chief Inspector said, waiting for the noise levels to die down. 'After a thorough search of the River Lee Navigation, uniforms have found nothing. There is one bit of good news, though. A male suspect was spotted close to *Kingfisher* shortly before our arrival on the scene.' Cummins paused for effect before continuing. 'Last seen heading towards the A12 and Stratford, who was he?'

PC White raised a hand to speak, and Cummins acknowledged her. 'Yes, Sheila?'

'Do we have a description, Boss?'

'Around five-ten, wearing a black hoodie and tracksuit bottoms. He was carrying a large grip bag in his hand and seemed in a hurry.'

'Not a lot to go on.'

'I agree, but you might ask yourself what he was doing there at four in the morning?'

The Chief Inspector perched on the edge of a table and peered over the top of a pair of half-frame glasses. Dressed in a smart pin-striped suit, white shirt, and brogue shoes, he'd clearly been summoned to a progress update that afternoon. Not that anyone took much notice, as the majority of junior officers kept well clear of such meetings for fear of getting sucked in. This was the first team briefing concerning the Navigation incident, and MR1 was full. It was a large turnout, and everyone was eager to be involved.

Taking up front row seats were DCs Summers, Jones and Crawford, and behind them two female undercover officers involved in the Ambergate Court operations. Sitting directly opposite PC White was Colin Burton from forensics, along with a tall male officer Mason knew from Road Traffic. He'd had several run-ins with him in the past. Nothing serious, but the officer wouldn't think twice about handing you a speeding ticket if he thought you'd exceeded the limit. Even when driving a police car.

Close to the door with her back to the wall, he recognised the Crime Scene Manager, Pam Godwin. Dressed in casual trousers, blue blouse and matching shoes, Godwin was a stickler for detail and never missed a trick when running a crime scene. Considered by many to be the up-and-coming star on the team, she'd spent the past six months working alongside Special Branch on a child trafficking operation.

Peering around, it was then Mason spotted David Carlisle. Notebook in hand, the profiler was deep in discussion with Ted Andrews, one of the many old hands in attendance that afternoon. What they were talking about he had no idea, but it seemed a pretty intense conversation whatever they were debating.

'Okay,' said DCI Cummins, drawing everyone's attention back to the crime board. 'How long has *Kingfisher* been moored in her current location?'

DC Jones raised a hand to speak. 'She was spotted at Rammey Marsh lock about a week ago.'

Cummins' dark brown eyes narrowed a fraction. 'We need to pull a timeline together of Martin's last known sightings. Who saw what, where, and when?'

'What about forensics, Boss?' asked DC Crawford. 'Anything of interest shown up?'

'We're still working on it,' said Colin Burton, the senior forensic officer present. 'There is a huge amount of evidence to sift through, let alone taking a fifty-foot narrowboat apart.'

'What are the chances of fast-tracking some of the more important evidence through the lab?' Mason asked.

'It's already in hand, Sarge. Apart from a large suitcase found stuffed inside the narrowboat's engine compartment with Harold Watkins' fingerprints all over it, we've since discovered a few bags of white powder which have been taken away for testing.'

'Interesting,' said Cummins. 'What was inside the suitcase?'

'Household items mainly. Electrical goods, camera, an old wall clock––'

'What about a gold watch?'

'No, nothing of that nature.'

Cummins was silent for a moment or two, as if lost in thought. 'This testing that forensics are carrying out, any idea of time?'

'We're hoping to have our first results within the next couple of hours.' Burton's frown lines tightened. 'What is of significant interest, though, is that we're currently examining a possible murder weapon. We know our suspect wore rubber gloves during the attack but were hoping to find minute traces of the victim's blood on it.'

'Is this the narrowboat tiller handle we found on *Kingfisher*?' asked Cummins.

'Yes. It is.'

'Good. Let's hope you find a match.'

Almost home and dry, Mason thought, as he jotted "potential murder weapon" down in his notebook. Next, he stared at the waterways map for some moments and tried to take in the bigger picture. From what he could see, the Lee Navigation ran from rural Hertfordshire all the way down to the River Thames and the heart of London. It was a picturesque and unbroken landscape with a cycling route running the entire length of the navigation. Looking at the detail, its meandering course made it a perfect environment for slipping in and out of society unnoticed. He made a mental check and closed his notebook. If forensics could prove beyond all reasonable doubt the tiller handle was the murder weapon, it would make life a lot easier. But that wasn't all. If the artefacts found inside the suitcase had Harold Watkins' fingerprints all over them, the case against John Martin was growing.

'What else do we know about Martin?' asked Cummins.

David Carlisle was quick to react. 'I've been doing some digging around, going back over old records involving road traffic offences. Ten months ago, John Martin received three minor driving convictions from the Sussex Police. Speeding fines mainly – nothing serious. What is of significant interest, though, is when I tried to delve back in time, a Terrence Lovett's name kept popping up.'

Cummins' grin broadened. 'Has Martin changed his name by any chance?'

'It would appear so.'

'Umm. That is interesting. What else have you uncovered?'

'Shortly after a Terrence Lovett was released from Wandsworth prison, he changed his name by deed poll. Why he chose the name John Martin I have absolutely no idea, but he obviously had good reason to.'

'So, that's how the bastard sneaked under the radar!' Mason interrupted.

Everyone sat stunned at the sergeant's sudden outburst.

Cummins face twitched with expectation.

'We've obviously been looking in all the wrong places, it would appear.'

'If it's the same Terrence Lovett, then too damn right we have,' the sergeant replied.

'Perhaps you could enlighten us,' said Cummins.

Right now, above all else, Mason was keen to get his point across. Shaking with anticipation he turned to face the assembled team. 'Terrence Lovett was a well-known wheeler and dealer, a man not to be trusted. Known throughout the West End as Mr Shifter, Lovett's main forte was selling stolen antiques to dodgy overseas clients. Back in the mid-eighties, he posed as a small-time antiques dealer in Portobello Road. Nothing flash, just your ordinary run of the mill stuff you can pick up in any flea market. It's what went on in the back room that was of major interest to the police. That's where the real expensive stuff changed hands, and all of it stolen to order.'

'How much are we talking about here?'

'When we finally caught up with Lovett, he was charged with the theft of antiques worth over a million pounds and given a twenty-year prison sentence.'

Gasps all round.

'So, Martin has previous?'

Mason laughed. 'The moment David mentioned Terrence Lovett's name, alarm bells were ringing in my head.'

The Chief Inspector grinned as he turned to Carlisle. 'Well done. We'll make a detective out of you yet, young man.'

'One day,' Mason jested.

Titters of laughter broke out.

'What else can you tell us about Terrence Lovett?' Cummins asked Mason.

As it all came flooding back, the sergeant scratched his head thinking. 'During the late eighties, Lovett was involved in a string of high-end antique robberies in the West End of London. Works of art mainly. Rembrandts, Turners, Constables, you name it they were all in the mix.' Mason shuffled awkwardly. 'Rumours ran rife that Lovett was linked with the Noonan "crime firm" at some point, but no one could ever prove it.'

'How come he was never picked up and charged with the offences?'

'He was certainly charged, but that's my point. When the police raided his house, they found nothing. It had all been salted away... and that's how Lovett ended up with the nickname, Mister Shifter.'

The room fell silent and you could have heard a pin drop.

'Hang on a minute,' said Cummins thinking out aloud. 'If Martin was given a twenty-year sentence back in the late eighties, how come he's out of prison so soon?'

'Bent barristers, Boss. The East End is full of them.'

'You've obviously had previous dealings with Mr Lovett,' said Cummins, shaking his head. 'What was your actual involvement in the case?'

'I wasn't involved,' Mason confessed. 'This all kicked off long before I joined the police force. It was station gossip mainly, canteen talk. The last I heard, Lovett had fallen on hard times and was dabbling in car boot sales and small-time auctions in and around the Croydon area. Nobody would touch him after he came out of prison, and who could blame them?'

'That would make sense,' Cummins said, turning to point at the crime board. 'Having given up on the antiques trade, Martin has since turned his hand to drugs.'

It took some moments to sink in properly.

'What about Martin's half-brother, Brian Fagan?' asked DC Herrington. 'Has he said anything to us yet?'

'Not since he was picked up and brought in for questioning, he hasn't.' Detective Andrews replied. 'The last I heard he was refusing to cooperate.'

Ted Andrews was the longest-standing member of the team. Tall in stature, with swept back white hair and long sideburns, he reminded Mason of a barrister's clerk he once knew. Polite and reserved, he genuinely liked the man. Not ambitious like some, Andrews was a plodder more than a go-getter. That said, if ever there was a person who could uncover John Martin's whereabouts, it was Ted Andrews.

Colin Burton, the senior forensic officer raised his hand to speak.

'Yes, Colin,' Cummins acknowledged.

'A quick update if I may. Apart from our initial drugs find, a recent search of Zelly's house uncovered a grip bag hidden beneath the bathroom floorboards. In the bag was a gun, rounds of ammunition, a quantity of cocaine and over four-thousand pounds in cash.'

Cummins exhaled through clenched teeth. 'Little wonder he's refusing to cooperate.'

'What about this grip bag the suspect was seen carrying earlier this morning?'

'Good point,' said Burton, 'but the suspect seen heading towards the A12 and Stratford was carrying a large bag – more like a holdall. This one is small.'

'Even so, the evidence must point to one of them being involved in Watkins' murder,' said Andrews thoughtfully, 'which one is the question?'

Carlisle screwed his face up as if something was niggling him.

'Martin's modus operandi certainly fits. A ducker and diver by nature, he's someone who doesn't stay in one place too long. A narrowboat fits in with his lifestyle perfectly, as it gives him the freedom to move around unnoticed.' Carlisle cupped a mug of coffee in thought. 'Martin is a loner by nature and will resist mixing with people. Hence his change of name.'

'What about his half-brother, Zelly. Is there a strong family bond between them?'

'I wouldn't have thought so,' Carlisle acknowledged. 'Martin will have few friends. I'm positive of that.'

'Now we're aware of the family connection, will they try to contact each other?'

'I doubt it,' Cummins cut in. 'That's the last thing they'd want to do.'

Mason smiled. 'Then we charge both of them with Harold Watkins' murder.'

Cummins nodded. 'Yes, I can agree with that.'

'Hold on a minute,' said PC White, thoughtfully. 'What about this firearm found under floorboards in Zelly's flat?'

'That's a bloody good point,' Crawford agreed.

Unconcerned by PC White's comments, Cummins looked at his watch. 'Okay, there's plenty to be getting on with. Let's meet again tomorrow morning – ten o'clock.'

It was agreed. Although they still didn't have a firm plan of action in place, no doubt Cummins would be working on one. The bottom line was, if they were ever to catch John Martin, they would need a stroke of good luck. Even so, nobody in their right mind would harbour a potential murderer. Not when accessories to murder usually received half the prison sentence the principles faced. Which begged another serious question: who killed Harold Watkins?

Mason stared at his notes, then circled "potential murder weapon." It would all come down to forensics, it seemed.

CHAPTER NINETEEN

Jack Mason clearly needed another drink. At home with his wife Brenda after another long day at the office, he was exhausted. Now that Brenda's overnight hospital bag had finally been packed, he was beginning to feel anxious. Rubbing bleary eyes, he tried to think positively. He knew that neighbours would be keeping an eye on his wife whilst he was at work, which gave him some comfort. It wasn't the best of arrangements, he'd be the first to admit, but he couldn't come up with a better plan.

In many ways, Mason was pleased the pregnancy process was nearing an end. Brenda was having a rough time of it lately, and he felt sorry for her. She lacked energy and getting out of a chair was becoming a real effort nowadays. Not an ideal situation, not in the circumstances it wasn't. He'd done all he could, but the thought that a new baby could arrive at any moment had frightened the living daylights out of him. What if he couldn't get to a phone in time? What if he was miles away chasing after John Martin?

His mind running amok, he poured himself another generous measure of whisky and tried not to dwell on it. The problem was, he'd never been in this kind of situation before. He'd tried talking to colleagues about it, but many were reluctant to talk. Men were strange creatures when it came to discuss their personal experiences surrounding childbirth, and he was far from impressed by it all.

'What's new at the zoo?' Brenda asked, lifting her head from a book she was reading.

'Nothing much,' he replied.

'Have you managed to find this gold watch you've been searching for?'

'Not yet we haven't, but we're close.'

'I thought you would have found it by now.' She paused for a moment. 'This Chief Inspector Cummins whose praises you keep singing, what's his involvement in all of this?'

'He's in charge of the investigations, dear, and he's a good man to have around.'

Mason briefly told her the latest developments, but Brenda was having none of it. She was worried about being on her own when the baby came along and had every right to do so. No wonder he was losing sleep. If they didn't catch Martin soon, how would he get time off work?

He decided to change tack.

'There's a new TV drama starting at nine o'clock, and the critics have given it rave reviews.'

'I'm more interested in this narrowboat down on the River Lee Navigation. What else can you tell me about it?'

The ominous tone in Brenda's voice cut through him like a surgeon's knife. He'd been working far too much overtime lately and was never at home when she needed him. He felt trapped, a product of his own success, and wished he'd thought this through. The truth was his promotion to Detective Sergeant had come at a most inconvenient time and there was nothing he could do about it.

'There's not a lot to say.'

'Really?'

'It's newspaper hype – journalists clutching at straws.'

'It doesn't sound that way to me. Whoever was living on this narrowboat seems to have disappeared.'

'Yes, but it doesn't mean they're guilty of anything. There could be all kinds of reasons why they've left.'

'Well, that's not what the papers are saying. They suspect it has something to do with this Clapton Park murder.'

'You know what journalists are like, I've banged on enough about them in the past.'

Brenda eyed him with suspicion. 'If you didn't think it was true, then why go to all the fuss of cordoning off a large stretch of the Navigation?'

'It's standard procedure, darling. That's what we're trained to do. You can't just let any Tom, Dick and Harry go wandering around a crime scene, it doesn't work like that.'

'So, it is a crime scene?'

'Well, yes and no.' Mason swallowed hard. 'We're still in the early investigatory stages.'

Brenda put her glass down on the coffee table and thought about it. 'The trouble with you Jack, is you're too engrossed in your work and it's beginning to affect your health. You're not sleeping at all well at night and you're constantly stressed out.'

Shit, Mason cursed. He was digging a hole for himself and Brenda was filling it in as fast as he could empty it. Yes, it had been a long day. And yes, he would have dearly loved a nine-to-five job right now. But that wasn't possible, not whilst John Martin was still on the run.

Mason tried to change the subject. 'What did the hospital say?'

'Not a lot, why?'

'Did they give any indications as to when Bambi is due?'

'Any time now.'

'Let's hope they're right––'

'You can't pick and choose the time and place to have your baby, Jack. It doesn't work like that!'

'No, I suppose not.'

His phone rang and Brenda nearly jumped out of her skin.

'Sorry, darling.'

He answered it, but all he could hear was a buzzing sound. He checked the display – number withheld.

Strange, he thought.

Brenda glared at him. 'One of your work colleagues?'

'I've no idea. Whoever it was they've hung up.'

'I hope they're not going to call you out in the middle of the night again.'

'I doubt it.'

Brenda glared at him. 'The sooner your suspect's behind bars the better.'

Mason afforded himself a rare smile. Truth out, he drifted into the kitchen to make some tea. Not that he particularly wanted one, he just needed some breathing space. Too many distractions were rattling around inside his head and it felt like a juggler balancing too many plates. God forbid there'd been another development. Not now, not tonight of all times.

'One sugar, or two?'

'Better make it one,' Brenda replied.

He poured some hot water into a mug and placed the kettle back on its stand. Life in the fast lane wasn't all it was cracked up to be and he was constantly searching for answers. He'd worked on some difficult cases in his time, but none with the pressures of this one. At least he had a new addition to the family to look forward to, but uncertainty was dragging him down. He would need to ease back, take his foot off the gas and come up with a better plan. Whatever that might be….

CHAPTER TWENTY

Mason had thought about ringing Brenda when his desk phone suddenly sprang to life. It was lunchtime, and he knew a friend would be calling in at home to check on his wife. Anxious, he'd not stopped thinking about her all morning. Grabbing the phone off the hook, he was surprised to hear a man's voice on the other end of the line.

'It's me, Sarge. DC Andrews.'

'How can I help, Ted?'

'Were you expecting an important phone call? You sound stressed out.'

'I thought it was the wife,' Mason replied. 'The baby's due any time.'

'I can't help you with that, but I can tell you there's been another incident.'

'Shit,' Mason cursed. 'Where are you now?'

'Near Walthamstow Wetlands. I'm down on the River Lee Navigation.'

'What's happening exactly?'

'An elderly man was fishing close to one of the lock gates when he thought he heard his car being broken into. When he went to investigate, that's when he was clobbered over the head.'

Mason jotted down some notes. 'What time was this?'

'He was found an hour ago, a mile south from where *Kingfisher* is moored.'

'Crikey! How is he?'

'Not good. The ambulance has just arrived and he looks in pretty bad shape.'

'Has he given a description of his attacker?'

'No, he wasn't able to. But he did say his attacker drove off in a southerly direction.'

'Mason thought for a moment. 'Do we know what model or make his car was?'

'It's a silver Ford Sierra, and it's fitted with a black roof rack.'

'That shouldn't be too difficult to track down.'

'I wouldn't have thought so. That said, we've put out an all cars alert.'

'Good man. We need to get forensics down there, and quick.' He looked at his watch. 'It's essential we secure the crime scene. Get uniforms involved – nobody to move in or out of the area without proper authorisation.'

'I'm on it, Sarge.'

'I'll be with you as fast as I can.'

With all thoughts of his pregnant wife now a million miles from his mind, Mason was keen to get going. Crime scenes had a nasty habit of quickly turning cold on you, especially if the evidence was tampered with. If this was

John Martin's doing, there was every chance of catching up with him. He grabbed his notebook and keys and took off in haste towards DCI Cummins' office.

Mason wasn't the only one who saw his weekend fast slipping away from him. Everyone else involved in the case would feel the same way too. Such was life. Nothing was ever straightforward.

CHAPTER
TWENTY-ONE

Jack Mason's biggest concern was securing the crime scene from contamination. This was a particularly vicious attack that had all the hallmarks of Harold Watkins' murder. But DC Andrews was a competent police officer, and Mason had every confidence in his ability to do a good job. Despite all the recent setbacks, the sergeant was feeling upbeat when he slid into the unmarked police car. Information that forensic scientists had found minute traces of Harold Watkins' blood group on the narrowboat tiller handle, gave him encouragement. They now had a murder weapon and it was a matter of matching it to the killer.

Blue spinner lights flashing, Mason watched as the traffic up ahead pulled over. The A107 was busy, with long tailbacks at every junction. Here he was, lunchtime, chasing his own shadows as yet another pensioner lay fighting for his life. It wasn't good, and a heavy media involvement wasn't helping either. Damn maggots, every one of them. Where did they get their information from?

Determined to take control, Mason parked up behind a stationary 4X4 BMW and sat in silence for a moment. He knew the area well and was familiar with its layout.

Through the bare trees and close to the lock keeper's house, he could see an ambulance was facing south with its rear doors flung open. Now a hive of activity, the rural tranquillity of the Lee Navigation had been well and truly shattered.

Met by DC Andrews, Mason wasn't relishing the idea of questioning a badly beat-up pensioner. His main focus of attention was pulling together hard facts and establishing a link to Harold Watkins' killer. A piece of discarded clothing or a footprint left at the scene. It didn't take much, and an overwhelming number of criminals made a mistake at some point or other. It was a matter of staying vigilant.

The sergeant stood for a moment, thinking.

'How is the old man?'

'It's not looking good,' Andrews replied. 'He's suffered blunt force trauma to the back of the head and has lost a lot of blood.'

'Sounds familiar,' Mason sighed. 'Let's hope he pulls through.'

Andrews nodded, but said nothing.

'Anyone see or hear anything?'

'Not that I'm aware of.'

'Pity.'

They stopped at the towpath close to the lock keeper's house and stood for a moment. He wished Andrews had had something more concrete to report, something he could get his teeth into. Mason hated this type of crime, as it always left him feeling irritable. Once forensics had finished their search of the area, hopefully they'd have a lot more to go on. He'd dealt with car theft before, many times, but this car theft felt much different.

'Who called it in?'

'One of the waterway workers. . . he was on his way to work when he saw the old man crawling on hands and knees. He was bleeding heavily and badly shaken up.'

Close to a bend in the river, just off the beaten track, Mason's attention was drawn to a small knot of people. He could see a trauma-team doctor holding up an IV bag, whilst giving instructions to a young female paramedic on the other end of the drip line. These things could never be rushed, it was a matter of holding your nerve and hoping the victim would pull through.

'Did the victim hear or see anyone acting suspicious before he was attacked?'

'God, no. He crept up behind him, I suspect.'

'Sounds about right,' Mason groaned.

Andrews, who was a good few inches taller, stared at Mason. 'He's obviously suffering concussion, but the paramedics should be able to tell us more.'

'Another premeditated attack, do you think?'

'The evidence points that way.'

Mason stood for a moment. Fifty yards south, he noticed the victim's fishing line still propped on its stand. It was a beautiful setting, an ideal location for a spot of quiet fishing. Not that he knew much about the sport, but it did have a certain appeal. Patience was his problem, as he didn't have any. His were more adrenaline sports, something to get the juices flowing. Not just sitting and waiting for a fish to take the bait.

Nearing a gap in the trees, Mason could see a small team of forensic officers hard at work. Stretched out in an extended line, he guessed this was where the victim's Sierra had been parked. Not anymore. It was probably a million miles away and stuck in a secure lockup. Further afield, uniformed officers had taped off a small area close to the Navigation. The ground underfoot felt hard and it hadn't rained the previous night. At least something was going in their favour, as it meant that most of the evidence hadn't been washed away.

DCI Cummins joined them at the water's edge.

'What have we got?'

'A badly beaten up pensioner, aggravated car theft, and no sign of our suspect,' Mason dutifully replied.

Cummins swivelled on his heels and pointed in the general direction from where he'd just come. 'I saw the ambulance... I take it he'll survive?'

'Hard to say at this stage, Boss.'

Mason filled in the gaps, and Cummins jotted everything down.

'Is this Martin's work, I wonder?'

Mason paused in thought. 'I'm not convinced.'

'Oh. What makes you say that?'

'Watkins' killer was a professional and knew what he was looking for. He came prepared, no forced entry, no fingerprints, and little in the way of physical evidence.' Mason kicked the soil from under his feet. 'The person responsible for this attack is an opportunist in my opinion. Apart from the car, nothing else was taken.'

'But he was disturbed in the act, and the method of attack was very similar to Watkins' murder. Blunt force trauma to the back of the head.'

'Whoever he is, he'll not get far as we've set up a couple units to cover the main artery routes.'

'Don't hang your hat on it, Sergeant. He's probably changed the number plates by now.'

Mason lowered his head in submission. 'There's always that possibility, of course.'

As DC Andrews took off towards the lock, Cummins turned to Mason. 'Brian Fagan, aka Zelly, is due before the magistrates at three o'clock this afternoon. Owing to the seriousness of the crimes we expect he'll be sent to prison until a trial date is set. Just on the off chance that Martin decides to return to Zelly's property, his phonelines have been tapped and we've set up a round-the-clock surveillance team to keep an eye on the flat.'

'I can't see Martin turning up at Zelly's place, Boss.'

'Why the negativity, Sergeant?'

'What, you think he'll return?'

'If he does, at least we'll be ready and waiting for him.'

Mason sighed. 'Finding Martin will be like looking for a needle in a haystack.'

'At least we know what we're up against, and we need to prepare for every eventuality.' Cummins shot Mason a glance. 'When's the baby due?'

'Any time now.'

'Excited?'

'Yes and no.' Mason felt his frown lines tighten. 'The wife's hospital bags are packed, but it's like sitting on a ticking time bomb and waiting for it to go off.'

'Who's looking after her whilst you're at work?'

'The next-door neighbour is during the day, and a couple of Brenda's friends keep popping in after work.'

'Let me know if you need any time off.'

'Will do, Boss.'

Cummins rocked back on his heels. 'I remember when my first son was born, it was a pretty stressful time. The trouble with being a police officer is, criminals tend to know when you're faced with family problems. That's when it usually kicks off.'

'Tell me about it.'

'You're a good police officer, Jack, and have a bright future in front of you. The trick is to strike an even balance between family life and work. Nobody is indispensable in this job, so don't overstretch yourself. Do that, and it will all come crashing down on top of you.'

It was sound advice, and Mason knew it. Not that he would take much notice. They were close to catching their killer and the thought of someone else stepping into his shoes was like waving a red flag to a bull.

No way Jose!

CHAPTER TWENTY-TWO

Mason sat in the passenger seat as DC Crawford drove. They were pursuing a silver Ford Sierra heading west along the A11 towards the capital, reaching speeds in excess of eighty miles per hour. As the needle continued to climb, Mason cast a critical eye over the route map calling out familiar landmarks along the way.

'Church at the next junction.'

'Which way, Sarge?'

'Left at the traffic lights.'

Foot hard on the brakes, needle dropping rapidly, Crawford's body language stiffened. As the undercover vehicle swung left, they were met by a stream of oncoming traffic. Most vehicles pulled over at the first sign of their blue flashing lights, but some didn't, and it was testing Mason's patience.

He spotted the getaway vehicle.

'Ford Sierra two hundred yards up ahead,' Mason eagerly announced.

'I see him.'

Seconds later, the car radio spewed out another load of undecipherable instructions as they climbed a short hill. They were looping west to where a stinger had been set in place, but the sergeant wasn't hopeful. Mason clutched the door handle as Crawford, always too heavy on the brakes, slammed his foot down, skidding erratically across the road as he turned hard.

'Christ Crawford, we want to catch the car without crashing.'

'Sorry, Sarge.'

Mason clenched his jaw. He hated being the passenger, especially when Crawford was driving. The risks he took made Jack feel like he was in an episode of Wacky Races.

'I've lost him again. Which direction did he go?'

'Right at the next fork in the road,' Mason anxiously replied, 'and easy on the brakes!'

Crawford hit the accelerator hard as the needle continued to rapidly climb. Ninety, one hundred, they were passing Bromley-By-Bow doing a hundred and five. Then out of the corner of his eye, the sergeant spotted flashing blue lights in his wing mirror. There were three of them in total, including a Vauxhall Cavalier SRI which was making easy work of closing the gap between them.

'Looks like the cavalry's arrived.'

'Christ! He's giving it some wellie.'

'God help anyone who pulls out in front of them.'

Within seconds, the Cavalier's grill was up close and intimate.

'Tosser,' Crawford yelled, banging the steering wheel in an angry show of contempt, 'Who does he think he is. . . Stirling Moss?'

Mason checked his wing mirror again. At first it didn't register, then it did. No wonder they were eager for them to pull over.

'Let them through, Bob,' Mason insisted.

Crawford glanced at the sergeant gobsmacked. 'What?'

'They're part of a tactical pursuit team and keen to close on their target.'

'But he's still in our sights.'

'Just do as I say.'

As Crawford's grip on the steering wheel slackened, so did their speed. Within seconds of moving over, three marked police vehicles shot past them at speed.

'What now?'

'Try keeping up with them––'

'What, with this heap of shite?'

The car's radio crackled into life.

"Driver of the stolen vehicle is believed to be John Martin. Firearms presence requested."

Mason checked their position. It was always policy in armed pursuits to use marked police cars where possible. With a minimum of three cars, if you could get in front and behind a speeding vehicle and box it in, there was every chance of stopping it. At least, that was the theory, and he was about to find out.

Mason could clearly see three marked police cars close on the Sierra's tail, too close for his like. Approaching a fork in the road, the Sierra unexpectedly veered right under a cloud of white smoke. For a moment, the world seemed to stop, freeze, then it was all sound and action again. At first, everything happened in slow motion. Then, through the haze of confusion, two marked police cars collided with one another.

'Right, right, right!' Mason screamed.

'The bastard––'

Now the lead pursuit vehicle, up ahead the Sierra's brake lights gave off an ominous red glow. They were heading down a long narrow street with shops on either side, and their speed had rapidly dropped. It felt surreal, unnatural, as if Martin was about to give himself up.

Mason recognised the used-car showroom up ahead and immediately hit the seatbelt buckle to decamp. But something wasn't right, something had spooked him, and he quickly fastened it again. This wasn't the safest place to carry out a Tactical Pursuit and Containment, not at any time. There were too many people around, too many side streets, as if the killer was luring them into a false sense of security.

'What the fuck?' Crawford yelled, as Martin began to accelerate.

'He's heading for the shopping centre.'

'What the hell is he doing?'

'We're driving down a one-way street,' Mason shrieked, 'and going in the wrong direction.'

'I know.'

As they squeezed through the narrowest of gaps, both wing mirrors exploded into a thousand pieces. Martin was desperate to get away from them, but acceleration was far too dangerous in such a heavily congested area.

Then out of nowhere a bright orange delivery van bore down on them at speed. Horn blasting, headlights flashing, it was straddling the middle of the road.

'Holy shit,' Crawford screamed out.

Mason braced himself for the inevitable.

CHAPTER

TWENTY-THREE

Mason's heart was in his mouth. His chest was hurting like mad, and he was suffering whiplash. No doubt his seatbelt had saved him from serious injury, along with the airbag which had exploded on impact the moment they hit the safety barrier. In what had been a combination of quick thinking and good fortune, it was a miracle that no one had been killed.

Dazed, the sergeant looked around. There was glass everywhere, and mangled vehicle parts strewn far and wide. He had been in dozens of car pursuits in his career, but nothing as hair-raising as this. To his left, smoke was escaping from beneath the orange delivery van's crumpled bonnet. It wasn't much, but he knew vehicles could catch fire. Even so, a short, stubby man in his mid-fifties had climbed into the driver's cab and was attending a man's bloody head wounds. To his right, a smartly dressed woman in a green checked coat was peering in through the Sierra's passenger window. She was young, mid-twenties with long blonde hair, and carried an air of authority that told him she knew what she was doing. She turned, signalled for assistance, then stepped aside to allow people to move in.

Was Martin alive?

The moment his police training clicked in, Mason pushed all thoughts of pain aside and turned to Crawford.

'You okay?' Mason asked, concerned.

'I think so, Sarge,' the constable replied. 'But I can't feel my legs.'

'I'll get some assistance.'

A curious onlooker poked his head through the vehicle's shattered windscreen and quickly disappeared. Who could blame them? If you couldn't stand the sight of blood why bother to get involved? Earlier in his career Mason had spent time as a Road Traffic Officer. It was all part of his training, and he loved every minute of it. Thinking back, picking up the pieces of a head-on collision was always his biggest nightmare – he hated it.

Still groggy, the sergeant slid from the passenger seat and stood for a moment. The High Street resembled a war zone. What started on a garage forecourt in the centre of Stratford, had ended in a multi-vehicle pile-up near Mile End Road. No longer his problem, the entire operation had been run from a command centre and the officer in charge would be answerable. There would be many times in the weeks ahead when he would relive Martin's irresponsible actions. It was a reckless piece of driving, an unforgiveable act of gung-ho selfishness. He took a deep breath and tugged on the driver's door.

It was jammed.

He glanced around for help.

It was then he noticed John Martin slumped over the driver's wheel. Eyes firmly shut, his face had a spectral appearance as if he were dead. Then his worst nightmare imaginable…

'Fire!' someone yelled.

Concerned for his colleague's safety, Mason heaved once more on the driver's door but still it refused to budge. He started to panic; petrol and flames didn't mix. All around him people were shouting out garbled instructions. No one was in control anymore, and panic was spreading.

'Help me! Help me!' Mason shouted. 'I'm police! Help me here!'

A group of onlookers rushed to Mason's assistance.

As the driver's door gave way, they gently eased Crawford out of the unmarked vehicle and away from imminent danger. In what was a race against time, he now turned his attentions to Martin.

Don't let the bastard out of your sight – the voice in his head kept telling him.

Terrified the Sierra might explode at any moment, Mason eased one arm behind Martin, wrapping the other around his chest.

'Help me pull him out,' Mason ordered the onlookers assisting him.

Still conscious, someone managed to free Martin's legs and Mason pulled.

Within seconds of easing Martin out through the driver's door, the engine erupted in flames. Many feared a terrorist bomb had gone off, but it wasn't that kind of explosion. As people dived for cover, the whole area was gripped by panic. Now fearing the worse, Mason spotted a tall man dashing out of a hardware store. He was carrying a fire extinguisher tucked under his arm, and a female assistant was struggling with another. Everything was moving in slow motion again, even the sounds were muffled. On reaching the flames, the two shop assistants worked in unison. First, they aimed their hoses at the seat of the fire, then pulled the extinguisher pins and squeezed the triggers. In what had been a quick-thinking act of unselfish bravery the fire was quickly put out.

Mason heaved a sigh of relief.

If there was a silver lining to the sequence of unfolding horrors, it was that he'd come out of it mostly unscathed. Yes, he'd been badly shaken up, and yes, his head was in bits. But the adrenaline had kicked in and was giving him a surge of energy.

He watched as two police officers involved in the vehicle pursuit began moving everyone back. Arms extended like human barriers they were desperately trying to bring a semblance of order to the proceedings. But they'd taken their eye off the ball, and Martin had spotted his opportunity. Scrambling to his feet, the killer ran straight towards a large group of onlookers. Nobody challenged him – nobody knew who he was – apart from the two uniformed officers now hard on his tail.

Still keeping an eye on Martin, Mason noticed the killer was limping heavily and his shirt tail flapped in the breeze as he ran. They would need to cut him off before he reached the network of waterways that criss-crossed the River Lee Navigation. Mason's biggest concern, if he could think of one, was that his suspect would have plenty of contacts he could call on – fellow criminals with a natural hate towards the police.

Mason gave chase.

On reaching the main shopping precinct, despair gripped him. The two police officers following in Martin's wake had lost their man in the myriad of side streets. It was all too much to contemplate; his brain wasn't fully functioning, and Martin was getting away from them. He stared in awe at the large group of onlookers they were attracting. Despite all the frustration, dozens of uniformed police officers had joined in the chase. It wouldn't take much, and with this number of officers at their disposal, there was every chance of recapturing their suspect.

Then the penny dropped.

Of course! Why hadn't he thought of it before?

Martin was heading for the underground and the labyrinth of tunnels within. He turned, pushed through the throng, and made towards the nearest station.

Just you and me now, John!

CHAPTER
TWENTY-FOUR

His neck hurting like mad, Mason ran down the stairs two at a time and almost lost his footing. Deep inside the bowels of the London Underground, he was having to rely on his instincts. It wasn't the best of situations to be in. Alone, no backup, and a man who wouldn't think twice about killing him. Warily, he strolled down the crowded platform, looking at every face, checking every alcove. He knew he was here. He sensed it. Hiding amongst the crowd and desperate to get away from him.

Mason felt a blast of hot air on his face as another underground train entered the station. Everything felt fragile, like he was walking on eggshells. As the train drew to a halt, he waited for the doors to open before checking along the carriages. The front of his white shirt was smeared in blood, and his suit spattered in engine oil. He looked like he'd been in a fight, and people gawped at him as he passed by.

Then, out of the corner of his eye, he spotted Martin. He was goading him through one of the carriage windows and challenging him to make his move. Two doors. One choice. Whichever door he entered, he knew Martin would alight from the other.

Feign entry – the voice in his head kept telling him.

The moment the train door alarm sounded both men made their move. But that wasn't all, there was something else that had caught Mason's attention and he couldn't quite put a finger on it. The next thing he saw, after he stepped back from the slow-moving train, was Martin screaming and the flailing of arms. Confused at first, a whole mix of different thoughts ran through Mason's head.

Unable to free himself, Martin's coat had snagged in the doors and he was slowly being dragged under the moving tube train. The minute someone activated the emergency alarms the driver applied the brakes. The noise it made was deafening, but three of the eight coaches were already in the tunnel by the time the train came to a standstill.

Seconds later a smartly dressed middle-aged man rushed to Martin's aid. He stopped, turned, and started to throw up. What damage had been done to the suspect's lower limbs Mason dreaded to think. But human bodies were good at dealing with trauma, he knew that from previous accidents he'd attended. If the emergency crews were careful when freeing him from his entrapment then maybe there was a chance.

Fighting his fears, Mason steadied himself as he moved towards the platform's edge. One look was enough. Crushed between platform and train, Martin's lower legs were missing and the flesh had been torn from his thighs. It was hanging in bloodred ribbons and he did not want to look any further.

Joined by the station manager and his female assistant, the sergeant instinctively made his position known. Martin was in such a state of shock that he didn't realize the severity of his injuries.

'What happened?' The stationmaster queried.

'He lost his footing.'

The stationmaster gave Mason an authoritative nod. 'I'll close the station down and alert the emergency teams.'

'Good man,' Mason replied.

'Is there anything else we can do?'

'You can move these people back before the emergency crews arrive.'

'Yes, of course.'

Arms fully extended, the stationmaster and his assistant began moving everyone back towards the exit staircase. It would take a good fifteen minutes before the emergency services arrived and he was hoping the ambulance crew would show first. If nothing else they could inject Martin with morphine to alleviate the pain. Even though the bastard didn't deserve it.

In the eerie dim light, Mason leaned over to check the suspect's pulse. It was then he spotted the Vacheron Constantin gold watch. It was attached to Martin's wrist, and the sergeant could barely contain himself. His immediate reaction was to walk away from it all and let the emergency services deal with it, but knew he could not do that.

He let go of Martin's arm.

'Soon you'll be dead, my friend and your miserable half-brother Zelly will be locked away for the rest of his life.'

The killer was gulping the air in snatches. It wouldn't take much, and the moment the emergency services freed him from his current entrapment he would die from hypovolemic shock. Blood dribbling from of the corners of his mouth, Martin was fighting it every inch of the way. He knew he was dying, knew he only had minutes to live, but still he refused to acknowledge the fact.

Mason heard footsteps approaching.

It was David Carlisle, and he was sprinting headlong towards him with two uniformed police officers close on his heels. The profiler looked pale, as if he'd seen a ghost.

'You okay?'

'A few bumps and scratches, but otherwise I'm fine.'

'I was--'

Mason turned sharply. 'How the hell did you find me down here?'

'They were lifting Bob Crawford into the back of a waiting ambulance when he told me you'd gone after Martin. When I reached the High Street, one of the officers told me you were heading this way.'

Mason eyed Carlisle with suspicion. 'How is Crawford?'

'Apart from a broken ankle and a few nasty cuts, he's fine.'

'Good. That is a relief.'

Carlisle drew back the moment he caught Martin's head poking above the platform.

'Crikey! How did this come about?'

'He was desperate to catch a train, apparently.'

'Is he alive?'

Mason narrowed his eyes a fraction as he turned to Carlisle and explained. He was reliving the memory again. The screams, the flailing of arms, and the moment Martin slid from view. Justice had been served, but it wasn't the kind of justice that Mason had been hoping to administer.

Carlisle took a closer look.

'Good God!'

'I know, and the bastard's wearing old Harold Watkins' gold presentation watch,' Mason said, angrily.

'So, it was him?'

'Terrence Lovett, aka John Martin, was extremely good at throwing other people off his scent. That's how he kept out of prison all this time. . . he knew how to play the system.'

'The cunning sod.'

'Just because you change your name by deed poll doesn't mean you're exempt from your past catching up with you.'

Carlisle nodded but said nothing.

'It was down to good honest police work in the end, and hundreds of hours of trampling the streets in search of answers.'

Carlisle stood to face the sergeant. 'Killers are made not born, Jack, and Martin is no exception. Once greed takes hold, anything is fair game. Martin is a magpie. If he fancies something, anything, he grabs it regardless of the misery it may cause.'

'So, you think this was all about greed?'

'Antiques runs through Martin's veins,' the profiler went on. 'Once he saw the watch, he knew he had to have it. Whether he intended to kill the old man in taking it is another matter, of course.'

'He intended to kill Watkins all right, that's why he went armed to his flat.' Mason hunched his shoulders as a cold chill washed over him. 'Zelly's the catalyst in all of this, that's why Martin relied so heavily on his half-brother's thugs to silence the estate.'

'Sounds like the two of them are in it up to their necks.'

'Absolutely. But no man's life is worth a price of a gold presentation wristwatch – no man on earth.'

Seconds later, two paramedics arrived on the scene, closely followed by a team of fire officers carrying what looked to be hydraulic jacking equipment. Trailing in their wake was a short stocky man in his mid-forties. Dressed in a Hi-vis jacket with Accident and Emergency Doctor splashed across the front of it, he was panting heavily and decidedly short of breath.

The doctor bent down and searched for Martin's pulse.

'Too late. He's gone, I'm afraid.'

Mason smiled. 'Well, that's one less problem to worry about.'

Carlisle looked at the sergeant gobsmacked. 'Hell, you don't pull any punches.'

'It comes with the territory, my friend.'

Carlisle said nothing.

As more emergency teams began to arrive on the scene, Mason felt the burden of responsibility slowly diminishing. It was time to touch base, report his findings back to DCI Cummins. At least he had some good news to tell him at last.

'We need to get this checked out,' the doctor said, pointing at Mason's headwound.

'Later, Doc. I still have a few lose ends to tie up.'

On reaching the main ticket hall, a group of senior transport officers were discussing future plans. It was mid-afternoon, and thousands of commuters would soon be arriving at the station. Looking decidedly harassed, the Station Master seemed eager to get his trains moving again, and who could blame him. But fatal accident investigations couldn't be rushed; there were procedures to follow, and not until a Transport for London manager had completed his findings could the station be reopened.

Mason turned to Carlisle. 'You were right about one thing. You always said he would strike again.'

'It was in his nature to do so. These people enjoy inflicting terrible suffering on vulnerable victims... they get a real buzz from it.'

Mason's phone rang, and he answered it.

It was Brenda.

'It's me, Jack. My waters have broken and the baby is on her way.'

'Where are you now, darling?' the sergeant replied, anxiously.

'I'm with Bella from next door. We're in the back of a taxi on our way to the hospital.'

His phone went dead.

'Shit!' Mason cursed. 'The sodding signal's gone and dropped out.'

'Bad news?' Carlisle said, showing concern.

'It's Brenda. She's finally gone into labour.'

Soon to become a dad, Mason was eager to be at her side.

Nothing more could be done for John Martin now, and it would be a while before the trains were back up and running again. Besides, there were more important things on his mind and Mason was desperate to get going.

***

On reaching the main station concourse, Mason contacted DCI Cummins and brought him up to speed with the latest developments. Instructed to stay put, within seconds of pocketing his phone a marked police car drew up alongside the station's main entrance.

He walked towards it.

'DS Mason?' the officer in the passenger seat asked.

Mason flashed his warrant card through the open window and stepped back a pace. 'That's me.'

'We've been instructed to take you to hospital, Sergeant.'

'Yes, to the University Hospital, maternity ward, as quickly as you can.'

Mason slid into the backseat of the vehicle feeling decidedly groggy. At least he was heading in the right direction for once and that's all that really mattered.

'Are you sure it's not A&E you want?'

'No, it's definitely the maternity ward,' Mason replied. 'My wife's gone into labour and I'm about to become a dad.'

'Maternity Ward it is.'

The moment they joined the steady stream of traffic heading west, the officer in charge switched on his blues and twos and moved to the outside lane.

'Nice one,' Mason thought, as the traffic up ahead pulled over.

It felt good being a Detective Sergeant for once.

CHAPTER TWENTY-FIVE

Holding his daughter for the very first time had been nothing like Jack Mason had ever experienced before. Part of him could not believe that she was actually in his arms, it was a miracle. He'd done some macho things in his time but nothing had tested his manhood as much as becoming a dad. He'd read all the books, mentally prepared himself for the occasion, but still was as nervous as hell when his daughter screamed her head off in the middle of the night.

Still on paternity leave, Mason was more than happy to get stuck into the housework. He'd learnt how to use the washing machine, change a vacuum cleaner bag, and cook the odd meal without having to rely on the microwave oven. It hadn't all been plain sailing, of course. There had been a few mishaps along the way. His biggest regret was burning a hole in one of Brenda's cotton sheets when he was ironing. He should have known better, but he'd taken his eye off the ball after his daughter, Claire, had distracted him.

These past two weeks had flown by, but Mason was missing the camaraderie, the buzz he got from putting the bad guys away. Although he'd made a lot of new friends at the station, he'd formed a special rapport with David Carlisle. They worked well together, got things done, which suited Mason's way of dealing with crime perfectly. Carlisle was a lateral thinker, nothing phased him. Or so the sergeant believed.

Mason couldn't always make things happen the way he wanted them to, but he was slowly warming to Carlisle's unconventional approach to problem solving. Not that he was into criminal psychology or the behavioural patterns of serious offenders, but it did have its merits. On reflection it had been a strange couple of months. So many questions, so many facts that didn't add up. He'd been right about one important aspect though: find the watch and it would lead them to the killer. Now it was rightfully back in the Watkins family, Mason was more than chuffed with the final outcome. The last he'd heard, Harold's grandson was proudly wearing it and never took it off his wrist. A chip off the old block.

Above all else, Mason had stuck rigidly to his personal promise – *never rush into things until you have all the facts*. The more he thought about it, the more his impending appearance at the Coroner's hearing on John Martin's death was becoming a mere formality. Now a clear-cut case, according to a spokesman for the Rail Accident Investigation Branch (RAIB), Martin had died as a result of an accident after stepping off a tube train. It wasn't the ideal outcome to a murder investigation, but at least the evidence was irrefutable and that's all that really mattered in the courts.

He heard a knock at the door and answered it.

Surprised to see Bob Cummins standing there, he immediately spotted the large bouquet of flowers he was carrying. White lilies, Brenda's favourite. How could he have possibly known?

'May I come in?' the Chief Inspector asked, by way of introduction.

'Who is it, darling?' Brenda called out.

'It's my boss, DCI Cummins,' Mason replied.

'What's up now, I thought you weren't due back until Monday, Jack?'

Cummins poked his head around the living door and smiled. 'It's purely a social visit, Mrs. Mason. I was in the area and thought it prudent to call by and see how you all were.'

Brenda blushed as Cummins handed her the bunch of white lilies.

'Goodness. They're beautiful.'

'How are the two of you keeping?'

'We're absolutely fine.'

'May I?' Cummins said, pointing towards their daughter's carrycot.

'Yes, of course,' Brenda replied.

'She's beautiful. I do hope I haven't come at an inconvenient time?'

'No. Certainly not. I've heard so much about you these past few months, it's nice just to put a face to a name.'

Cummins took up a seat opposite and stared over at their daughter's cot again. 'How's Claire settling in? Has she managed to take over control of the house yet?'

Mason lifted his eyes to the heavens as if to emphasise the point. 'How did you guess? She's a demanding little bugger and has the voice of a Sergeant Major at times.'

Cummins laughed out loud. 'Most do at that age, and it doesn't get any easier, I can assure you. I remember our first son, he clearly knew how to gain our attention the first few months of his life. There were times, and quite a few might I add, when we thought he'd never stop crying. At one point, Janet and I were thinking of taking him back to the hospital in exchange for a quieter model.'

It was Brenda's turn to laugh.

It didn't take long before their conversation got around to the latest news coming out of Hackney Central Police Station.

'Just for the record,' said Cummins, casually, 'we've charged Brian Fagan aka Zelly as an accessory to murder. The CPS are hoping for twenty years, but it's far too ambitious in my opinion.'

'How long, do you think, he will get?' Mason asked.

'Hard to say. At least ten years, by which time Clapton Park will have hopefully moved on.'

'I did hear something about that on the news,' Brenda said. 'What about the other gang leader? The one who tried to stab, Jack. What's happening to him?'

'Tony Abbott,' Cummings acknowledged. 'He's charged with wounding Paul Siddons, along with ten other knife related crimes. Abbott's a dangerous felon who thought he was untouchable. Not anymore. He too is facing a very long prison sentence, as are many of his so-called gang members.'

Brenda thought for a moment. 'Hopefully that will put a stop to it all?'

'I fear not, sadly. No sooner do we take one gang off the streets than another pops up in its place.' Cummins sighed, as if to make a point. 'It's a never-ending cycle, and there is no simple answer, unfortunately.'

Mason shrugged. 'One day, Boss.'

'Yes. But not in my lifetime sadly.' Cummins stood to leave. 'It's been lovely meeting you, Mrs. Mason, but alas duty calls.'

'Thank you for dropping by, Chief Inspector.'

'As my wife fondly reminds me, a policeman's work is never done.'

'I can certainly vouch for that,' Brenda smiled.

Reaching the hallway, Cummins turned at the door. 'There is one other thing. Your informant from Tower Hamlets, Peter Daniels. How helpful was he?'

'Boss?'

Cummins tilted his head to one side. 'As I remember we handed him five hundred quid of hard-earned police funds for information leading to the watch.'

Mason's mind raced.

'Ah, yes.' The sergeant hesitated, knowing full well that Cummins had warned him about using informants as they often sold your information on. Truth be known, Daniels hadn't even bothered to contact him. 'Shall I say his service was very beneficial.'

'Good. Not like some of the scumbags I know who take your money and run!'

Mason groaned inwardly having learnt another valuable lesson.

Cummins turned on his heel. 'We'll see you on Monday morning then?'

'I'm looking forward to it, Boss.'

'Oh! Before I forget, Superintendent James sends his regards.'

'That's very considerate of him?' Mason said, confusedly, somehow turning the statement into a question.

The Chief Inspector rolled his eyes. 'Another major assignment has landed on his desk, but it's all very hush-hush I'm afraid. He's holding a meeting about it on Tuesday morning, and wants you to attend.'

Mason's brow corrugated. 'Did he say what it's about?'

'Not to me he hasn't.'

'That's odd. I thought he would have said something.'

'What I can tell you is, that you and the profiler David Carlisle will be working a lot more together in the future.'

'Does this have something to do with Tuesday's meeting?'

Cummins made a little grimace. 'No doubt the Superintendent will fill you in with all the details.'

Keen to get back into the swing of things, Mason wondered what the future might hold. The thought of another major assignment excited him, but not the mountain of paperwork that went with it. Mason hated administrative bureaucracy at the best of times, and forms were the bane of every police officer's life. But they were still an important administrative necessity.

The moment DCI Cummins closed the door behind him, Mason's mind was all over the place. Whatever it was his boss was holding back on, he was desperate to find out.

'What's happening at work, Jack?' Brenda asked the moment he entered the room.

'Not a lot. There are a few loose ends I need to tie up on the Watkins case, other than that it's back to the grindstone as usual.'

Brenda put her paper down and looked at him oddly. 'What's so important about this hush-hush meeting on Tuesday? Why all the secrecy?'

Mason had no answer to that.

THE END

YOU HAVE TURNED THE LAST PAGE.

But it doesn't have to end there . . .

Why not check out Michael K Foster's author website at www.michaelkfoster.com and subscribe to his newsletter.

Here you will find behind the scene interviews, discount promotions, signed book giveaways, and more importantly new release dates.

If you enjoyed Hackney Central, why not drop a review on Amazon and let other readers know what you thought of it. They are dying to hear from you!

THE WHARF BUTCHER (#1)

When Jack Mason is called to a brutal murder scene at an isolated farm in Northumberland, his worst nightmare has become a reality. Two people are dead, their bodies lie twisted and broken, but nobody knows why.

The pressure mounting, the clues don't add up. Far too many people are entangled in this crime – some with dark secrets to hide, others unwilling to cooperate. When things take an on unexpected twist, Jack fears a serial killer is at work and a criminal profiler is brought in to assist. But this killer makes his own rules and draws them ever closer into his twisted web.

A chilling psychological suspense thriller set in the rugged North of England, The Wharf Butcher is the first book in this gripping new series that will shake you to the core.

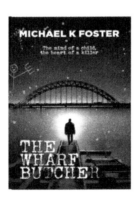

'Start to finish, the author hardly gives you time to catch your breath as horror piles on horror and the killer thumbs his nose at the pursuers.' *The Northern Echo.*

SATAN'S BECKONING (#2)

(Book 2) In the DCI Mason & Carlisle Crime Thriller Series

When a fatal road crash turns out to be murder, JACK MASON is sent to investigate. There are no clues, no motive, and the driver of the car is missing.

Within the seemingly dark vaults of the police missing persons files, lay untold dangers. Young women are easy pickings for a serial killer who is growing increasingly audacious. When criminal profiler DAVID CARLISLE is drafted in to assist, he is not able to protect anyone – least of all himself.

As the investigations intertwine, Jack is forced to face his own demons, but the closer to the truth he gets, the greater the danger he puts them in.

Satan's Beckoning is a fast-paced crime thriller with a cliffhanging conclusion.

'An outstanding writer of considerable talent and with this, his second novel he has proven yet again that he is a new force in British Crime Fiction.' ***Booklover Catlady Reviews.***

THE SUITCASE MAN (#3)

(Book 3) In the DCI Mason & Carlisle Crime Thriller Series

When DCI Jack Mason is sent to investigate a gruesome double murder, his entire world is turned upside down. The ex-wife of a notorious gangster lies dead, a second victim's body is missing, and the evidence doesn't stack up. A few days later, when a young man's body turns up hidden inside a city storage locker, the head and hands are missing.

With Jack's powers of investigation tested to the limit, a criminal profiler is brought in. But, the inner workings of this killer's mind won't be easy to decipher. In a world of human trafficking, drugs, and gangland unrest, who can Jack trust?

'... The plot and dialogue are top-notch which move the reader forward effortlessly. Gangland unrest, drugs, and human trafficking and suspense make this book a must for anyone who enjoys the genre. The Suitcase Man is the third in the series, however, can easily be read as a stand-alone novel in its own right.'   *The Book Worm.*

THE CHAMELEON (#4)

(Book 4) In the DCI Mason & Carlisle Crime Thriller Series

It was meant to be a harmless adventure...or so the boy thought.

When a ten-year-old boy playing hooky from school sees a young woman's body hanging from a tree, a man at the scene gives chase. Still recovering from near fatal injuries, Jack Mason is sent to investigate. He knows the boy's life is in danger, but that's the least of his worries. There's a much darker side to this investigation, and one that threatens to change many people's lives. What really happened in the woods that day? What dark secrets was the dead woman hiding? And who, or what, is Chameleon?

You will be hooked from the start by this gripping crime thriller. There's tension, suspense, and a plot full of unexpected twists and turns. Order your copy today.

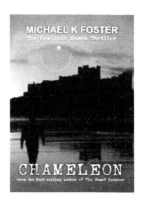

'Once again the author has delivered another gripping tale of murders that leaves the reader wanting more. Very believable, gruesome, well written and engaging to the end.' **Dan Brown.**

A LETTER FROM MICHAEL

Dear Reader,

I hope you enjoyed reading 'Hackney Central.'

A question readers often ask is where my ideas come from. The simple answer is, they come in many guises. Let me explain. Whilst searching for new material for my next novel in the current crime series, I stumbled across a pile of old research notes concerning Jack Mason's early years when he served with the Metropolitan Police. Little did I realise that twenty years later my initial thoughts would be turned into a full-blown bestselling crime thriller series.

Set in the nineties, London's notorious East End was a hotbed of serious crime, but it also suffered deep poverty, overcrowding, and associated social problems. The closure of East End Docks in the Port of London was undoubtedly a major contribution, but the socio-economic changes in what came to be known as Thatcher's Britain, only exacerbated the situation.

Brought up on a rough council estate in London's East End, at age six, Jack Mason's father walked out on his mother leaving them virtually destitute. Life was tough, but after knuckling down and studying hard, he managed to scrape through his police entry exams to join the Metropolitan Police.

Known as a no-nonsense copper, he soon caught the attention of his superior officers. It was this, and a natural talent for detective work that quickly earned him the rank of Detective Sergeant.

Dispatched to the notorious East End of London, Jack's tough upbringing would hold him in good stead during those early years. No stranger to trouble, he quickly gained a reputation amongst the criminal fraternity for his hard-hitting tactics.

In Mason we are dealing with a deeply flawed character, and readers are drawn to him for many reasons. Unbending, impulsive, and driven, many of his plans are back of the cigarette packet affairs. An extrovert who draws energy from people and hazardous situations, many see in Jack Mason what they see in themselves – one of life's fighters.

Thank you again for choosing to read my books!

Michael

Printed in Great Britain
by Amazon

23230060R00108